Naalaayak 2 Laayak

OrangeBooks Publication

1st Floor, Rajhans Arcade, Mall Road, Kohka, Bhilai, Chhattisgarh 490020
Website: **www.orangebooks.in**

© Copyright, 2024, Author

All rights reserved. No part of this book may be reproduced, stored in a retrieval system, or transmitted, in any form by any means, electronic, mechanical, magnetic, optical, chemical, manual, photocopying, recording or otherwise, without the prior written consent of its writer.

First Edition, 2024
ISBN: 978-93-6554-461-9

VeKiKuNe

OrangeBooks Publication
www.orangebooks.in

Dedicated

To my Lord who ordained me to this work. I am always indebted for this opportunity.

"Sreerastu Subhamastu Avighnamastu"

My Prayers for your uninterrupted reading devoid of distractions

Index

Part I: The Caterpillars 1

    There's one in many homes. 2

    Meeting Of Like-Minded Professionals 14

Part II: The Pupae 70

    Everything is a hypothesis 72

    What do you do with them? 87

Part III: The Butterflies 125

    Seeing through the lens of others? 127

    Alignment to the Vision 161

    Justice delivered 165

Part I:
The Caterpillars

Foreword.

To put things in perspective, nearly twenty million adolescents in India are being added to the addiction list annually. The primary substances of abuse include liquor, opioids, cocaine, amphetamines, and hallucinogens. The government has rolled out several initiatives, such as the National Action Plan for Drug Demand Reduction (NAPDDR) and the Nasha Mukt Bharat Abhiyaan, to address this crisis through preventive education, awareness generation, and rehabilitation programs. Unfortunately, voluntary enrolment in de-addiction centers has decreased since 2020 following the COVID-19 pandemic.

The main causes of addiction—environmental factors, stress, mental health disorders, availability, and emotional pain—are creating an ever-expanding clientele for these substances. This escalating trend has dire consequences for national health, growth, and reputation. Our ancestors employed other means to manage stress. These individuals are always intoxicated and do not contribute anything to the society they live in.

These individuals, often labeled as 'Naalaayaks,' are the protagonists in my book.

It is not compassion or empathy that's driving me to consider the 'Naalaayaks' as my protagonists but rather a hope that this book will lift their spirits and rekindle their hopes.

My only hope is that my message gets to my audience either directly or indirectly, and they will pick this book, read it, and do what is necessary to be labeled as Laayak.

There's One In Many Homes

1 At 6:00 a.m., a small two-bedroom home is filled with commotion. A husband and wife in their late 40s rush not to miss the city bus, striving to avoid retribution from their bosses. According to the monthly roster, the husband, a warehouse keeper at a timber depot, must relieve the night shift worker. His wife, dedicated to her job, provides elderly day-care for an aged couple. In their haste, they remain oblivious to their son, Vinay, who sleeps undisturbed despite the high-decibel preparations.

In his late teens, Vinay operates in a time zone +12 hours apart from his parents. He enters the home when they are asleep and exits before they return from work. The photos hanging in the living room are the only reminder of a family once close-knit. Vinay grew up in an environment lacking ample care owing to the economic rhythm of their parents. His youthful photos depict a bubbly and charming boy, but now, he's a young adult with a cold demeanour.

His parents sacrificed having a second child to shower all their love and resources on one sapling. Yet, in the absence of guidance during his formative years, Vinay took advantage of his freedom, drifting away unnoticed.

His friends Sharath and Bhaskar also come from families with similar struggles.

There are many Vinays, Sharaths, and Bhaskars in the streets who gather around the cafeterias, viling away time.

With a heavy heart, Swati carries a steaming cup of coffee to the older man, her employer, pleading for help in finding a way to settle her son, Vinay. The older man shrugs at her request and, with a touch of exasperation, calls Vinay "Naalaayak."

"I can't do much for your son," he says. "He lacks the etiquette of speaking to elders and disregards good advice. Only God can help you and your son."

The word "Naalaayak" stings Swati deeply, but she cannot contest it. Knowing it holds a truth; she dares not challenge it.

Peer pressure to match materially and inflation led to the necessity for both partners to earn. In pursuit of happiness, they have prioritized the principles of capitalism over familial morals.

2 Just a few blocks away, in a family more affluent than Swati's, lives a young man who begins his daily routine. Kiran packs his laptop, hangs his ID card around his neck, and grabs the keys to his newly bought KTM bike. He seems like a happy young man with everything going for him for the outside world. However, behind his smile lies a hidden pain.

Part I: The Caterpillars

He's an average coder, lucky to have a small job, but he constantly faces his boss's tantrums, who labels him a "Naalaayak." "You couldn't complete a simple program on time, and your work has many logical mistakes. I spend my whole life teaching you basics. Look at Ravi and Chandu; they're so good at their work." These constant comparisons have taken a toll on his self-image.

He feels out of place, forced into a career that doesn't align with his true passion for landscaping. The societal pressure to conform has led him to a life of obligation, leaving his talents and dreams unfulfilled. Watering plants in the morning, he envies the flourishing roses under his care blooming. That is the only time he feels accomplished and satisfied yet aware of the toxic workplace, where he will spend a third of his day deeply wounded. The word "Naalaayak" haunts him even in his dreams, draining his energy and leaving him dragging his feet to the office daily. This constant burden of judgment and failure looms over him, overshadowing the moments of peace and fulfilment he finds only in caring for his beloved plants.

3 In the dimly lit lockup of the local police station, a young lad finds himself in a dire state. Caught in a police raid, Shiva and his partners in crime were consuming contraband. The intoxicants still wreak havoc on his system, leaving him weak and dehydrated.

Circle Inspector Naresh strides into the station, greeted by the customary salutations from his officers. He takes his seat and listens to the debrief on the previous night's raid. With a heavy sigh, he summons the "Naalaayaks," but his dismay grows as he sees they can barely walk coherently. Deciding to take matters into his own hands, Naresh walks up the alley to the cell where the young men are confined.

As he looks at their faces, a wave of melancholy washes over him. These young lads, barely out of their teens, remind him painfully of his son. The stark contrast between their lives and his son's path strikes a deep chord within him. He feels helpless, as any sermon would only fall on deaf ears, and any corporal punishment will not help either. He resigns, advising his staff to collect the demographics and contact their parents.

The police team identified the individuals by validating their fingerprints against the Aadhaar database, as they could not reveal their identities due to their condition. This is a customary practice to see if fingerprints can solve some petty crimes from the past. They have summoned their parents, expecting them to arrive shortly.

Shiva's widowed mother, however, was non-responsive. She couldn't bear the thought of facing the Circle Inspector, having lost all hope in reforming her son. This was a trauma she faced for the second generation. "The fruit can't be any different from its seed," she thought, resigning herself to a life of continuous pity and despair.

Trembling, Swapna walks up the stairs of the Police station to meet the officer who called her and informed her of Shiva's plight. It is for the first time she is in this God-forbidden place. She walks up to the reception and enquires about his son Shiva. The officer asks her to meet the Head constable. After a brief wait, she gets the opportunity to meet the HC. HC was expecting a man and quizzed Swapna, and she had to reveal her marital status as Widow. HC starts recounting the felonies Shiva was caught red-handed. She couldn't believe her ears on the saga of Shiva. HC reprimands Swapna for being callous in his upbringing. Tears roll down her cheek with a sigh of helplessness.

She has to work in five to six houses to make ends meet. She leaves home even before the Sun rises and toils till afternoon, only to return with a broken back. She barely has energy left by evening and settles in bed early, only to follow the circadian cycle over and over again.

4 Within the same neighbourhood stands a plush bungalow with a sprawling lawn and two luxury cars parked in its portico. The occupants are a successful doctor couple: the husband, a renowned anaesthesiologist, and the wife, a busy gynaecologist. They have four support staff, including a home guard, a driver, and two full-time maids.

During their prime years, the couple were deeply immersed in their professions, often available even during odd hours. Consequently, they spent little time raising their only son, Vikram, who is now in his late teens. While they are materially well-off, their main concern is their wayward son, who couldn't succeed in the competitive exams to secure a medical seat. According to Plan B, they are considering sending Vikram to a private medical college in Georgia. However, his lifestyle remains a significant concern. The pampered young man assumes life will always cater to his whims, with entitlements that seem never-ending. This worries his parents, who fear that Vikram might not grasp the importance of hard work and discipline necessary for success in his chosen field without a drastic change. Vikram assumes his parents are a perpetual source of income, allowing him to enjoy life's comforts without much effort or concern. Unbeknownst to him, the support staff discreetly refers to him as "Naalaayak" behind his back. His sense of entitlement blinds him to the growing resentment and disappointment of those around him, including his parents, who worry about his future and the consequences of his attitude.

At 11:30 a.m., the familiar sound of the internal lift cranking to life signals its descent. This is the cue for the maid to prepare and serve hot coffee, defying the mother's wishes. The maids have kept this small act a secret to avoid any unnecessary retribution, knowing that the parents have already left for work by this time. It's a quiet rebellion, a gesture of kindness amidst the underlying tension in the household. With a heavy heart, the maid delivers the message from Vikram's parents, reminding him to complete his mock tests. He's supposed to present the results when they return late in the evening. As she reads out the to-do list prescribed by his parents, Vikram slowly turns his head, fixing her with a piercing look that serves as a silent warning to stop. The tension in the room is palpable, and the maid's reluctance is mirrored in the young man's growing frustration. She mumbles to herself, "What curse have these lovely masters been burdened with, ending up with this 'Naalaayak'!

5 Vikram takes a quick shower, slips into his wrinkled clothes, and grabs the keys to his Harley Davidson bike. He heads to a café to meet his best friend, Santosh, another pampered child of a real estate billionaire. Recently, they've noticed a decline in the number of sycophants around them who praise in exchange for favors, leaving them to grapple with a reality where their once-unquestioned entitlements are starting to fray. Many of their friends have successfully secured seats in engineering or medicine and are now immersed in their busy lives. This shift has left Santosh and Vikram feeling isolated. With a touch of bitterness, Santosh calls these friends selfish for pursuing their paths. Vikram, echoing this sentiment, dismisses them as suckers and opportunists, not realizing who is drifting in real. Santosh stands out in the crowd with his movie-star looks. At Six feet two inches, with a fair complexion, broad shoulders, and a flair for theatrics, he effortlessly impresses those around him. Fully aware of his charm, he seizes every opportunity that comes his way.

However, his distraction from studies began in high school, as he revelled in a steady stream of infatuations. He barely managed to pass the milestones, and his declining performance went unaddressed. His father was preoccupied with his business, and his mother was engrossed in maintaining their social status.

All his friends call Santosh "Naalaayak" on his back. They manage their time and prioritize, as their moral standards at home are different. If Santosh had grown up in one of their homes, his outlook on the world would have been different. Anyway, this is just a hypothesis, as there is no way to prove or disprove it.

 The security guard working at Vikram's bungalow is a migrant worker from another distant state in the late fifties. He is hired through an agency to keep a watch. He must keep a vigil at night, which leaves him tired from the daybreak. His shift ends by 9:00 a.m., only to return to work by 9:00 p.m. He is alone here, leaving a family of three others in the native village to keep a watch on his aging parents. He calls upon his wife twice a week just to check on the affairs at home. Listening to her, his pain only aggravates. He is constantly reminded of the income deficit and the hardships his wife is facing as a lone warrior woman. His grief is compounded by his inability to fulfill his roles as a son, husband, and father.

Last week, Shankar, his middle-aged son, was expelled by his employer for his callous attitude towards work, leaving the owner with considerable loss. This was his last opportunity to turn around and prove to be a dependable employee. Shankar has lost the count of his employers, and the maximum stability he demonstrated does not exceed 6 months. No one now believes in his sincerity. He suffers from a trust deficit among the villagers and is often referred to as "Naalaayak."

During Shankar's formative years, he observed his male relatives emigrating to the Middle East as laborers, finding better livelihoods abroad. The fear of moving away from the familiar confines of their village to distant, unknown places was a change his grandfather couldn't reconcile with. Shankar's father, defying this deep-seated trepidation, became the first person in generations to step out of the village, much to his grandfather's chagrin. His soul yearns to explore the world, but he's bound by the chains of restrictions imposed by familial moral fabric. The contrast between his dreams and reality underscores his profound struggle, caught between the desire for freedom and the weight of familial and societal expectations.

7 The opposition benches in the State Legislative Assembly are demanding an apology from the welfare minister for a remark he made on a community, brandishing all young members of that strata as "Naalaayaks." The Minister was unapologetic for his remark, which soon escalated to this situation.

The minister reads the crime rate and identifies a pattern proving his hypothesis. Though his choice of words is questionable, the conclusions of a recent Psychological Demographic study reveal an alarming picture of doom not far ahead. The opposition is concerned about the language, leaving the intent just to suit their political and appeasement agenda.

The Minister has a reform plan, but by the time he presents it, the benches are empty, and no one is there to listen. This kind of political drama can often overshadow important issues and potential solutions.

This episode has fed the media houses to organize live shows by evening calling politicians, thinkers, and reformers from Left to Right and initiating a street fight. As usual, they fan the emotions much to their liking as they feed their TRP ratings. They, too, are uninterested in the solution. The media houses are interested in sensationalism over substance. Media outlets often prioritize drama and conflict to boost their ratings rather than focusing on meaningful discussions and solutions. This can lead to a cycle where heated debates and emotional outbursts overshadow essential issues. It's frustrating when the real problems and potential solutions get lost in the noise.

While politicians and media remain engrossed in their battles for personal gain, the tragic story of 19-year-old Fatima, who died under suspicious circumstances, is forgotten. By the time the facts emerge from her community, they are filtered and twisted beyond recognition. Yet, the truth has a way of surfacing from the shadows.

Fatima, the youngest child of an octogenarian from his fourth marriage, dreams of a better life. Her father, a tailor with a small kiosk in a bustling shopping complex, struggles to support his family. The generational gap between Fatima and her oldest sibling is vast, and their conflicting aspirations often clash. In this case, the collision went too far. The entire community discredited Fatima's character to protect the perpetrator, branding her as "Naalaayak." However, an account from her friend reveals her aspiration to become an air hostess, showcasing her desire to rise above her circumstances.

Politicians and the Media are also "Naalaayaks." In situations like these, the real question is about justice and accountability. Labelling the victim as "Naalaayak" is not only unjust but also a diversion from addressing the actual issue—the perpetrator's actions. The victim's character should never be called into question as a means of shielding wrongdoing. Such ideologies and arbitrary interpretations rooted in outdated beliefs only serve to perpetuate injustice.

Bringing the perpetrator to justice requires unwavering commitment from the law and society to stand against such ideologies and support the victims. The true "Naalaayak" here is the one who commits the crime and those who perpetuate a culture of blame and shame on the innocent.

Politicians are busy in their pursuit of power, and the Media is busy with their TRPs, which leaves us to question who will take the initiative for reforms.

Part I: The Caterpillars

Meeting Of Like-Minded Professionals

❝────────❞

CI. Naresh is sipping coffee served by his wife on Sunday morning. He was glancing through classifieds for some property he wanted to invest. Suddenly, his eyes got fixed on a Title "Deaddiction Help Centres," promising psychological guidance for youth who drifted and were enslaved by the contraband. This wasn't new to him, but he saw a fresh angle in helping transform "Naalaayaks" into "Laayaks". He sees the address, and to his dismay, it is hosted within his jurisdiction. This advertisement was running in the back of his mind the whole day, and by evening, he had a plan in place to validate his hypothesis to check the veracity of this claim. "There are many quacks these days scamming gullible people; this shouldn't happen in my territory," he resolved.

He summons a home guard, Veeru, the next day and assigns him the task of keeping a vigil on the premises and informing about all the people who are visiting the office from daybreak till night for this week. He is supposed to report back with photos of the people and bear all care not to expose this clandestine operation. He wanted to be doubly sure that this was not another hoax meant to drain the resources from gullible citizens. The home guard was also entrusted to talk to some of the customers who walked in and gather information on the treatment's effectiveness, the charges, and the number of sessions required for the entire process. The Head Constable was instructed not to assign Veeru any other duties.

Veeru, a proven asset for such covert operations, ventures on the assignment immediately and starts his vigil diligently. He conducts reconnaissance of the premises and identifies that there is only one entry and exit point. The premise is on the second floor of a commercial building on a busy main street. The office opens around 9:00 a.m., with the receptionist being the first. She quickly cleans and dusts the reception area and sweeps the common corridor, placing the foot mat at the door.

For the first two days, there is hardly any movement except for the receptionist and a well-dressed personality, most probably, Dr. Ramesh, who enters around 10:00 a.m. and exits the office around 05:00 p.m. Veeru quickly concludes that the work will progress only if he lodges within the premises and gets a first-hand glimpse of the inner sanctum sanctorum. He devises a plan and executes it the next day.

He enters the office seeking any domestic help, including distribution of Pamphlets and other menial jobs. He introduces himself to the receptionist with an alias Abhi. The receptionist is just elated by the offer, as she was supposed to find an agency to distribute the advertising material. She asks Abhi to return at 11:00

a.m., and will have to discuss this with the proprietor, who is also a Professional Doctor in Clinical Psychology.

He spends time within the campus and, at Eleven sharp, enters the premises only to be greeted by the receptionist with a smile. She had discussed the job with Dr. Ramesh and got the go-ahead to hand it over for Rs. 200 per day. He negotiates and agrees to Rs. 350.

Abhi was very happy to get lodged on his first try. However, it is unclear to him where he can find the clientele who will instantly relate to the services that are being offered. He quizzed the receptionist, "Where do you think I should distribute?" Dr. Ramesh overheard this conversation. He summoned Abhi to the inner sanctum. Abhi deftly switched on the camera before entering.

The room is spacious, with a large wooden table in a corner facing the window. A luxurious leather recliner is in the centre of the well-lit room. This room alone occupies nearly 60% of the total office space of 800 Sq. Ft. There are file cabinets with security locks. There is a door to the left concealing a room from where the subject's relatives can oversee the conversation without being exposed. He is familiar with this setup that is present at the police station where he works. There are several unopened cartons as the premises have only recently been inaugurated. The smell of some puja performed within the office is still evident.

"Where have you worked earlier?" Dr. Ramesh asked, to which Abhi replied, "There is no standard place thus far

I have found. I have experience in the distribution of pamphlets in Mindspace Ad agency."

"Good, where do you think the mothers and wives of drunkards live? They are my clientele. They are the people who are most affected by this affliction. They are the people who are constantly seeking external help to get their husbands and children out of this quagmire".

"That's a wide space. I know many of them in my neighbourhood. Our ward never sleeps; there is commotion multiple times from midnight till daybreak. I can take you directly to the households and organize a Door-to-door campaign."

Dr. Ramesh smiles at his faith and orders him to get to work immediately. Veeru quickly finds an excuse, as his objective is to stay at the premises to observe and not leave it for one moment. "Those women return from their work only after 7:00 p.m.; until then, I can be of some use to you in the office." He offers help, hinting at cleaning and organizing the contents of the boxes.

Though initially reluctant, assuming Abhi is illiterate, Dr. Ramesh allows him to stay and help open the boxes and hand each content with care. Dr. Ramesh meticulously places the files bearing some code number in the same order as those handed over. The Doctor's discipline is evident in every detail, from the labelled boxes to the catalogued files. There are also several books and novels. Veeru's attention was fixed on a CD titled "Maro Prapancham" [Figure 3] from Volga Videos. Several other books are from 'Sri Sri' and other revolutionary reformists of yesteryears.

It was very unusual these days to stay away from peeping into their phones for long. "This person appears to be from a hermit kingdom, where no one has any distractions," Veeru muses to himself.

At 05:30 p.m. sharp, the Receptionist takes leave for the day, leaving only Dr. Ramesh and Veeru. Dr. handed over some change and summoned Abhi to get some tea and snacks for us both. Veeru returns in no time so as not to miss any opportunity for any activity.

The doctor opens slowly and starts questioning Veeru's neighbourhood regarding demographics, families, professions, youth, aspirations, etc. Dr. and Veeru both leave at 7:00 p.m., duly locking the premises and handing the second set of keys. The shutter has two sets of twelve-lever Safe locks on either side, which require two twists each. It is very clear that without the keys for the shutter and the sanctum sanctorum, it is impossible to break in unless the window of the office chamber is kept ajar.

Veeru peddles to the Police station with the bundle of Pamphlets that were supposed to be distributed to report back to CI. Naresh, who called upon him to update the progress.

By 09:00 p.m., CI. Naresh gets free and calls Veeru. Veeru gives a detailed account of the premises and individuals and shares the photos. CI quizzes him about the files, but Veeru has nothing to share beyond cryptic codes. When asked about his plan to gather more information from the files, Veeru reluctantly reveals his idea. CI listens and simply says, "You are on your own." Veeru pleads for CI's support if he gets caught in the act.

After the call, CI. Naresh takes his leave, and Veeru heads home. He places the pamphlets on the TV, cooks' dinner, and goes to bed. However, around midnight, he is disturbed by a commotion—a man in an inebriated condition creating a ruckus and engaging in domestic violence. Veeru can only be a spectator, as his hands are tied by the law, and his role in law enforcement is limited to reporting, not intervening. Sleep eludes him, connecting the dots. "Why on Earth is the Doctor interested in this type of clientele? What does he achieve by reforming these incorrigible folks? Where does he earn his living, as this scum has nothing to offer in return? What is hidden in those files? What is that book in red cloth so valued that it is placed under lock and key?".

Veeru, the day is set out again. The next forty-eight hours will be nerve-wracking for him; he must set the stage in the day and execute it in pitch darkness. Of all, he should give the doctor a debrief on the distribution progress. He picks up the bundle of pamphlets, removes a third of the leaflets, and ties it back. He cycles his way to the Police station and signs the attendance register, as it is customary if the home guard is not on Patrolling duty. He slips without being noticed by HC to avoid any distraction.

He cycles to the corner of the road from where the window is visible. Veeru is lean yet muscular, he was selected after proving his athletic endurance in the physical efficiency test comprising sprinting, obstacle clearance, etc. He calculates the length of the rope that is required to descend halfway from the fourth floor. "I must stabilize my weight by twisting the rope across the legs so that his hands can gain a grip on the window, allowing me to enter," he pondered to himself. He has to organize some fifty-meter three-inch smooth rope. He walks up the stairs to the terrace and is pleasantly surprised that the terrace entrance is unsecured. Even before venturing out on the open terrace, he peeps to see if there are any cameras viewing from the neighbouring building, which is hosting a cell phone tower. Confirming that there is no peeping tom, he walks to the side of the terrace with the designated window. "Where do I anchor the rope?" as soon as this thought ran in his mind, he found a square pillar a few feet away that could serve as an anchor. He assessed that figure Eight knot is best suited to hold a hundred kgs. A sandbag is required to reduce the friction on the edge of the wall and avoid wear and tear to the rope, risking snapping. With the approach plan finalized, it is time to build the alibi to bring in sand and keep the window ajar. Before leaving the terrace, he identifies the windpipe through which the foul gases accumulating in the plumbing escape. He pushes a plastic bag deep inside using a steel rod that was found on the terrace. This trick should block the leaking of foul gas and flush it back into the office spaces. "This is a big gamble; if it doesn't work, I will fall out of favour," Veeru pondered. After confirming that all possible scenarios were factored and satisfied, he descended the stairs, cautious that his movements go unnoticed even by the cameras placed strategically along the third and fourth-floor retail establishments. "Something is to be done to jam them at night," he thought. He will require something to distract the watchman of the Silver Jewellery store on the third floor or move like a cat without being noticed.

Veeru decided to take some rest and come to the premises around 11:00 a.m., when the drainpipe trick should have started working. He also needed to pick up the rope, the master key, the electronic signal jammer, and the sandbag to execute the plan.

Veeru called CI with a request to divert the Night Patrol at around midnight and keep them engaged for two hours. After a long silence, he heard a simple nod. That was enough cue to proceed.

CI. Naresh has chosen Veeru for one quality: he doesn't question "Why?" He carries out the instructions and brings the desired results in almost all circumstances.

Also, he is young, unmarried, and a First-Generation Urban migrant who came to this city with many dreams of making it big in the law enforcement department. His education is basic, but he is gifted with abundant survival instincts. He is detail-oriented in his approach and very cautious. He is also technology savvy; he knows many things about spyware, jammers, etc., and is up to date on matters related to electronics. These qualities make him a good spy.

Veeru returned to the premises fully prepared for every possible scenario that could possibly occur with an alternate plan. It looked as if everything was going to be smooth. Veeru greeted the receptionist while entering, only to be ignored. He tried to enter the office, but he was objected to as the doctor was with some clientele. This is the first time since the day recce has started. The office has good acoustics; even Veeru's sensitive ears couldn't pick up the conversation except for the occasional laughter. Guessing by the hoarseness of the voice, the other occupant must be a person in his late forties or early fifties. "Is he the clientele or friend?" quizzed Veeru. "How does it matter to you? Stick to your remit," came the curt reply.

Veeru picked the local newspaper and flipped pages. His eyes got fixed on the Headlines of the missing young adults in the city. The article's title was in bold, bordering on the fringe of sensationalism; it read something like "How long will the families of missing persons have to wait for justice to be served?". The photo of DSP. Prathyush Reddy, who is taking an application from the victim's family members, is presented in color. "Will I ever become the master in my lifetime?" Veeru envisioned, his emotions rekindled looking at the Insignia on the ironed uniform donned by DSP and the wand of law, the 0.5 caliber service pistol neatly ducked into the shining brown leather jacket. Expecting some praise for the arm of Law, he reads through the content. Bewildered by the lack of decorum the media has set out to use against the entire police fraternity; he was shocked and slightly agitated.

Suddenly, the calling bell rang, jolting the receptionist from her slumber. She quickly closed all the apps she was viewing and opened the door. Dr. Ramesh needed some incense sticks to be lit. Veeru couldn't suppress his smile but knew it wasn't enough. He had to amplify the inconvenience calculatedly to position himself in a consultative role, allowing him to take control of the situation.

"Are you also sensing that smell?" Veeru inquired.

"About what?" the receptionist countered.

He pointed her to the faint, putrid smell, hinting it might be due to a dead rat. He then suggested that rats might have come in during the shift and died there, unable to find food or an exit. Veeru's suggestion was so distasteful that it triggered equal parts dislike and fear. Feeling unsettled by Veeru's suggestion of rats, the receptionist unconsciously placed her feet on the chair to feel secure from the imaginary threat. Veeru's plan was working as the discomfort spread, creating the opportunity he needed to take control of the situation.

"Can I help in some way?" offered Veeru.

"How many things are you good at? You do one job perfectly well and don't present yourself as a jack of all trades", retorted the receptionist.

Veeru instantly concocted a list of various jobs he had done, including plumbing, electrical work, painting, and more. He thought he had lived all seven lives in this single life.

The receptionist demanded, "What have you done with the pamphlets? First, give the account. The Doctor may ask at any moment."

"I could only distribute about a third of them but ensured they had the right prospects. Very soon you will be busy managing long queues and a flood of phone calls. Your right hand will be holding the phone to the ear and left counting money". Veeru replied.

"Abhi, don't act overly smart. The clientele you distributed may not be able to read or write. I am not sure about the outcome of the path chosen. These days, social media is the way to catch attention. Everyone is glued there," the receptionist responded.

There is undeniable truth in what she was preaching. It had been almost two hours, and the clock struck at 1:00 p.m. The Receptionist rose from her chair, approached the door, and knocked twice. She opened the door gently upon hearing the confirmation from the other side. She spoke to the doctor to take a recess for lunch and inquired if anything was to be served for the inmates. The doctor questioned if Abhi was around and let him in; he wanted to run some petty errands.

"Yes, Sir, he has been here since morning. I will send him in".

With the door half open, she told Veeru to get in as the Doctor was expecting some help.

"This is a nice opportunity to see who is inside; he switched the spy camera covertly and entered the office room. It was difficult to resist a salute to the uniform. The figure was facing the doctor and couldn't be clearly seen. His shoulder signaled a person of DSP stature. He did not see the police caravan outside when entering the premises! Generally, there is a protocol vehicle and traffic police managing visits of some higher-ups in the neighbourhood. He thought that when DSP is here, CI. Naresh must be around. He quickly noted that he would not salute even if it was his boss and that exposing himself would jeopardize the chances of the mission.

"What will you have, Sir, Hot or Cold?" The doctor asked, extending the courtesies to the DSP.

"Nothing. Thanks for your courtesy. I have spent almost two hours here. I will have to leave now." DSP rose from his seat and, extending his hand to the Doctor, spoke the parting words, "It was a pleasure talking to you and sharing your views on the problem. We will be in touch. I will need your guidance and help solving the puzzle." Thus, the Police officer, none other than DSP. Prathyush Reddy, was revealed.

Raising from his seat matching that of DSP's stance, "You are most welcome, Sir. It will be my pleasure to be of some use to you in your pursuits. I Wish you the very best". He held the hand of DSP firmly one last time and accompanied him to the lift, discussing the next steps in discussing the idea he shared a while ago. DSP agreed to suggest some slots after looking into the calendar and promising his office would contact you regarding this.

Returning to his chamber, Dr. Ramesh found Veeru already there. As he walked to his seat, he coughed, the air thick with incense smoke. He ordered Veeru to open the window to let in fresh air.

"Shall I also open the bathroom door for better cross-ventilation?" Veeru prompted.

"No, no," the Doctor rushed to answer. "That's the source of the issue. I need a plumber to fix the problem."

Veeru was ecstatic as his plan was on track. "I do know some plumbing. Can I check the issue and see if I can fix it?" he offered.

With a curious expression, Dr. Ramesh asked, "If you are a plumber, where's your tool bag?"

Veeru replied, "It has been some time since I paused that line of work. I was always dealing with the more unpleasant parts of the water cycle and wanted to avoid being branded for a certain type of job. However, I do have a basic kit at home. I've installed bathroom fittings and solar geyser plumbing at many homes". He paused just to check if this much intro generated any interest.

While listening, Dr. Ramesh was trying to connect with someone over the phone. "The plumber who worked on the interiors has to fix it for free. He is obligated as his work is within the warranty period. He doesn't pick up my phone!"

"It may not be a big issue; maybe there's some vacuum created in the channel that's causing the reverse flush. If that's the case, I won't charge anything," Veeru offered, thinking his free help would be a good motivator.

"Chiranjeev, the plumber, is just like you. He is so good at making conversations; time flies by when he's around," remarked Dr. Ramesh.

Veeru faintly remembered Chiranjeev, who often came to the police station to fix the plumbing. If Dr. Ramesh managed to call him, Veeru knew he should avoid coming into direct sight.

Dr. Ramesh was about to hand over some cash, suggesting some petty work, when his phone rang, interrupting the smooth exchange. He picked up the phone with his left hand and pulled his right back to the table. Instantly recognizing the saved number, he answered, "Where are you, Chiranjeev? How soon can you come here? The bathroom smells like rotten fish, and the office chamber is becoming unbearable. I need you here quickly."

"Did you notice any water leaking after the flush? Is the water level in the toilet rising to the brim? Did you happen to push something through the commode?" Chiranjeev tried to diagnose the issue over the phone.

"No, I haven't used the toilet for the last two days. Why don't you come and see for yourself, instead of asking all these questions?" the doctor demanded.

"I am out of town, Sir. I can only come next week. Why don't you get someone else to fix it this time? I'll check on it when I return. I had to stay back at my native place for the festival and will be here for a few more days. I can suggest some home remedies if that helps," Chiranjeev explained, much to Dr. Ramesh's displeasure.

"Keep your suggestions. I have someone here who can help. Nevertheless, visit the office at the first possible opportunity upon your return and address the root cause. For now, talk to this guy and assess if he can fix it." saying this, the Doctor handed his phone to Veeru with speaker mode active.

"Yes, tell me", Veeru replied curtly. "Can you go to the bathroom and check a few things for me?" He took permission to enter the bathroom and close the door. He checked if the keypad sound was activated; luckily, it wasn't. This is a god sent opportunity to install spyware. While deftly delaying the answer, he spends time on the browser, logging into the spyware account and installing the client application. He answers with a nod for every ask just to confuse Chiranjeev and extend the direction of the diagnosis. It took three minutes to install spyware on the Doctor's phone. After evaluating all possible scenarios, Chiranjeev suggested handing over the phone to the Doctor.

"He seems to have some idea about plumbing, Sir; however, I cannot place him in my contacts. You may take his help for now. I will check on the same day I return." Chiranjeev ratifies the competency to the Doctor.

Veeru took permission from Dr. Ramesh to get his toolset and left the premises. Once outside, he quickly connected to the doctor's hacked phone, gaining access to contacts, messages, the gallery, and more. He then picked up his basic toolset in a cloth bag and returned to the premises.

Dr. Ramesh was impressed with the quick turnaround and started to trust Veeru. Around 2 p.m., Dr. Ramesh left for lunch at a nearby food court, allowing Veeru full access to the chamber, but not before ensuring all the lockers were secure. The receptionist, absorbed in her mobile, provided Veeru with the perfect opportunity to test the master key. Unfortunately, Veeru discovered that his master key didn't work, leaving him disappointed.

Upon returning, Dr. Ramesh felt very uncomfortable as the stink had worsened, making him feel sick. With no appointments scheduled for the rest of the day, he decided to leave the office early, around 3:00 p.m. and handed over the responsibility of closing the premises to the receptionist by 5:30 p.m. He instructed her to allow Veeru to do whatever he could before they closed for the day. Before leaving for the day, Veeru left the window ajar.

Veeru's plans were mostly successful, except for the Master Key. He went to a nearby hardware store in search of a lock and key like the ones used for the cabinets. He picked the one closest to the family of locks he needed to break open that night. After trying various methods, he found that a raw tool like a safety pin worked better than sophisticated tools.

As night fell, Veeru proceeded without a hitch. Moving stealthily like a cat, he avoided detection by the watchman on the 3rd floor. He secured the rope, placed the sandbag on the parapet, and slowly slid down the wall. Upon reaching the designated window, he quickly lodged himself inside and secured the thread, preventing it from swinging in the wind.

Veeru meticulously opened the lockers, spread the contents on the floor in the same order, and began taking photos with his phone. He set a strict ten-minute limit to complete the task to avoid attracting suspicion from the patrol party. In that time, he managed to take nearly a hundred photos, mostly of coded files. He then remembers the file covered in red cloth. He opens the cabinet and takes pictures of the dairy inside. Engrossed in taking pictures, he isn't worried about the content. Satisfied with his work, he quickly restored everything to its original state, wiped all traces of his presence, smeared some chili powder, and exited as smoothly as he had entered.

MAMUS: Double ka meetha

Returning home with his heart still racing from the high-adrenaline activity, Veeru quickly drifted into sleep. Before doing so, he sends the image of Mamus– Double ka Meetha [Figure 2], a dessert of the Deccan, a cryptic message to CI. Naresh: "MAMUS," which stands for "Mission accomplished, meet you soon"

Veeru knew the mission was nearing its conclusion, and he needed to place the capstone to ensure a proper wrap-up. With CI. Naresh is likely to release him back to normal duties starting Monday, and HC is expected to saddle him with backlogged tasks; Veeru had to effectively close the business with Dr. Ramesh. Abruptly leaving would jeopardize any potential future missions.

He planned to remove the obstruction in the windpipe and display a dwindling bundle of pamphlets, the primary reason for his employment. This would leave a good impression and maintain the integrity of his cover.

The doctor handed Veeru five hundred rupees instead of the usual three hundred and fifty, acknowledging the extra help with the plumbing issue. Veeru, ever the professional, tried to negotiate for a higher amount. "Take this hundred more and that's it. Don't expect any more from me now," the doctor said, winning the bargain.

As Veeru was about to leave, Dr. Ramesh registered his number in his phone as "Abhi handyman." This small gesture signified the doctor's growing trust and appreciation for Veeru's help.

Veeru felt a sense of accomplishment as he exited, knowing he had successfully maintained his cover while completing the mission. The doctor's gratitude and the extra payment were the perfect capstone to his efforts. Now, he could look forward to returning to his normal duties, ready for whatever new challenges might come his way.

Veeru vanished from the site, bidding a final adieu to the receptionist. She had been the key to the whole mission, and her desire to delegate the pamphlet distribution aligned perfectly with Veeru's objectives. Coincidentally, he had appeared at just the right time. As he walked away, he thanked her silently from within.

Veeru felt a sense of closure and satisfaction, knowing that his mission was complete. The receptionist remained unaware of the crucial role she had played, and Veeru hoped their paths would cross again under different circumstances.

Veeru peddled to the police station to report to CI. Naresh. HC's face turned red upon seeing him. "Look, the master of the station has arrived. Where the hell have you been the entire week? You will be paid only for twenty-three days this month, with seven days deducted for your absence."

HC grabbed the attendance register, ready to get it signed by CI. Naresh so it could be sent to the Accounts department before the cutoff day, the third Saturday of every month, to process the salaries. Veeru followed him into CI's chamber, gently closing the swinging gates behind him. Seeing Veeru, CI. Naresh signaled for HC to place the register and leave them alone. HC, upset by the CI's apparent favour towards Veeru, grudgingly complied, feeling overshadowed by the younger officer.

Inside the chamber, CI. Naresh turned to Veeru with a serious expression. "So, Veeru, how did everything go? Are we in the clear?". Veeru moved to CI. Naresh's side, showing him the prized collection on the phone. CI. Naresh took the phone and instantly recognized the value of the content. He ordered Veeru to transfer the files to a shared folder on the computer, which was hidden from plain sight and secured by the password '!nL2L#'" a cryptic message he had noticed on the Red File, captured in an image.

CI. Naresh carefully watched as Veeru transferred the content, knowing that these files held critical information. The atmosphere in the room was tense, filled with a silent understanding of the importance of their mission. With the transfer complete, Veeru stepped back, awaiting further instructions.

"You have sent 'Double Ka Meetha,' what's double about this?" CI probed, looking to understand the double bonanza of the mission. Veeru revealed that he had hacked the doctor's phone and could access his messages and gallery, and even track his whereabouts at will.

CI. Naresh was taken aback, contemplating, "Did Veeru go way too far?" The moral boundaries in the trade of spying sometimes bordered on civility. He understood the gravity of Veeru's actions and the potential risks and benefits involved.

The reward for Veeru's successful mission came swiftly. CI. Naresh called HC into the chamber and instructed him to correct the attendance, giving Veeru a full waiver. "The work he was assigned did not allow him to come to the police station, however, he informed me and that's enough proof that he was on the job," CI. Naresh explained.", and don't forget to give him the Deepavali gift hamper. We have enumerated home guards as well, right? Let him have my share as well".

HC, accustomed to following orders, made the necessary corrections to the file and prepared it for approval. He also handed the gift hamper. Veeru stood by a sense of accomplishment washing over him as he knew his hard work had paid off. The mission had been a success, and now he could return to his regular duties with a sense of pride and achievement. HC, with a subtle sense of vengeance, loaded Veeru with the backlog and even more tasks. However, Veeru, adept at handling pressure, managed to tackle the increased workload. His resilience and efficiency only further solidified his reputation within the station.

A few weeks passed, and the mission took a back burner, with the gathered intelligence collecting dust. CI. Naresh was caught up with other priority tasks. One unusually relaxed Saturday, he remembered the folder and called Veeru to get the coordinates and password. With complete access, he began to review the photos on the computer screen.

The numbered files included photos of individual patients, with their demographics, case histories, and complaints on the first page. The second page featured various Freudian hypotheses, some stricken out. CI. Naresh realized these were patient files but couldn't relate any of the photos to criminals under his jurisdiction. He knew he needed to assign this task to someone who could validate the information against a broader database.

Then he came across a series of photos that appeared to be notes scribbled in a diary enveloped in a red cloth. The cover had an iconography of Lord Ganesha with a punchline that read, "2nd chance for a better life." This immediately caught CI. Naresh's attention. The image of Ganesha, the remover of obstacles, paired with such a profound message, added a layer of symbolism to the doctor's work, suggesting a deeper intent behind his treatment of patients.

CI. Naresh pondered the implications of this mission and the ethical considerations it raised. He knew the delicate balance between gathering intelligence and respecting moral boundaries was challenging. With this newfound insight, he decided to delve deeper into the doctor's files to understand more about the enigmatic message and its significance.

The content was intriguing. He skimmed through the notes, noticing the title "Naalaayak 2 Laayak". The word "Naalaayak" was part of the lingo in their profession. CI. Naresh quickly drew parallels between his work and the doctor's, considering their contributions to society. He realized both of them dealt with the complexities and challenges of their respective fields, often dealing with individuals who were seen as "Naalaayak" or unworthy, yet striving to turn them into "Laayak," or worthy.

Part I: The Caterpillars

The diary notes revealed more about the doctor's philosophical musings and unconventional methods. CI. Naresh felt a curious kinship with the doctor, understanding that their approaches, while different, aimed at improving lives and bringing order out of chaos. This realization added a new layer of depth to the investigation, blending professional respect with a personal quest for understanding.

CI. Naresh downloaded two photos from the folder onto the desktop, opened them in the photos app, and cropped the boundaries to bring the focus in. Unaware that this approach would affect the resolution and cause pixelization, he saved the edited images, deleting the master copies from both the desktop and the recycle bin.

He then composed an email to the constable who had access to the central database, attaching the cropped images and requesting a search for any matching criminals in the database.

CI realized that each photo was a treasure trove of information, and he had barely scratched the surface. Thoroughly examining them would take time, and doing so at the station was impractical. He needed to find a way to transfer those files to his personal drive without violating the file share policy.

Knowing the risks, CI. Naresh decided to proceed cautiously. He planned to copy the files to an encrypted USB (B+C) drive, which he could securely access later from his personal computer or mobile. This way, he could analyse the data in detail without raising suspicion or breaching protocols.

Part I: The Caterpillars

CI. Naresh's thoughts were abruptly interrupted by a radio message alerting him to the DSP's entry into his territory from the South-West direction. He quickly swung into action, rising from his seat, adjusting his uniform, and picking up his hat, checking on his service revolver. His actions were carried out subconsciously, a demonstration of his finely tuned muscle memory.

Ready to greet the DSP, he left the room with an air of confidence, leaving behind the encrypted USB drive in his personal drawer and the yet-to-be-explored depths of the mission files. As he stepped out, he knew that his dual responsibilities—upholding his duty while navigating the shadows of espionage—were about to collide.

DSP. Prathyush Reddy's caravan, led by a pilot vehicle and followed by the station's jeep, arrived just in time. CI. Naresh rushed to open the car door for DSP. Prathyush Reddy. Upon exiting the car, DSP. Reddy gazed at the rusty police station board. He acknowledged the salute with a nod and said, "Vishraam," signalling everyone to relax.

CI. Naresh stood at attention, waiting for further instructions while ensuring everything was in order for the DSP's visit. The atmosphere was a mix of respect and anticipation, as the station's officers awaited their next directives from their distinguished guest.

DSP. Prathyush Reddy walked ahead swiftly, holding a polished bamboo truncheon in his left hand, signaling CI. Naresh to take the position on his left, aligning with the hand holding the stick. This subtle directive was a test of CI. Naresh's adherence to protocol and etiquette is a key aspect senior officers use to gauge the competence of their subordinates.

As they proceeded, the atmosphere was charged with a blend of discipline and anticipation. The officers in the station observed closely, aware that any lapse in protocol could reflect poorly on their unit.

DSP. moved to the chamber, asserting himself as the unit's boss during his stay. He gestured for everyone to stay outside except for CI. Naresh indicated he had important business to discuss.

"Relax, Naresh. I was just passing through this area and wanted to check on you as it had been quite some time. How are you? How is the family? Your son must be a young man by now. He was born when I was CI, and you were a Constable. I remember those days very well. Twenty years have passed since we worked as close as those days," DSP said with a hint of nostalgia.

CI. Naresh felt a warm rush of emotions. His respect and admiration for DSP. Prathyush Reddy were rekindled by their personal connection and shared history. The conversation brought back memories of their early days in the force and the camaraderie that had shaped their professional lives.

"By the way, congratulations for solving the murder case within 24 hours. I heard it in the Monthly Leadership meeting. Good work. So, what keeps you busy these days?" quizzed DSP.

"Thanks, Sir. I have developed a good team here, and the results are showing up. Unless I am transferred to another station or another post, I will continue to produce good outcomes for our department."

CI. Naresh and DSP spent a leisurely thirty minutes reminiscing about old times, creating a relaxed atmosphere. The staff listened in, amused by the easy camaraderie and noting how Naresh's achievements had clearly earned him respect. The fact that the DSP had chosen to visit Naresh in person rather than summoning him underscored the high regard in which he was held.

The DSP nodded approvingly, sipping the best tea and cookies that were served hot. "Excellent, I do not doubt your abilities. However, with the recent promotion opportunities, there's always the possibility of new challenges on the horizon. How's your team adapting to the new caseload?"

"They're handling it well, Sir. We've implemented some new strategies, and our collaboration has never been stronger. We're ready for whatever comes next".

"That's what I wanted to hear. Well, I came here to tell you that you are part of the newly formed task force I led. We need to solve a tough case and bring the perpetrators to Justice. There is a Kick-off meeting tomorrow in my office at 5:00 p.m. You will get an official email. I know you won't be late."

CI. Naresh's eyes widened slightly, a spark of determination igniting within them. "Thank you, Sir. It's an honor to be part of this task force. I'll be there promptly at 5:00 p.m., ready to tackle whatever comes our way".

The DSP nodded, a serious expression on his face. "Good. We're dealing with a complex web of clues and suspects. Your experience and intuition will be invaluable. Make sure your team is prepared as well. We'll need all hands on deck".

CI. Naresh straightened up, feeling the weight of responsibility but also the thrill of the challenge. "Understood, Sir. We won't let you down".

The DSP gave a final nod and turned to leave. "I'll see you tomorrow, Inspector. Let's bring these criminals to justice."

CI. Naresh accompanied the DSP to his car, exchanging smiles as he bid him a salute. He returned to his cabin, which had been tidied up except for a few untouched cookies. As he savored one, a sweet sense of anticipation filled him at the prospect of working closely with the DSP again. CI. Naresh became busy with his work but did not overlook the need to keep a reminder at 3:00 p.m. the next day just in case he forgot.

The Revealing Rendezvous

CI. Naresh had purchased two uniform sets beyond the ones the department provided, reserving them for special occasions. "I've got your Suit #3 ready," his wife called through the bathroom door as Naresh showered. The night before, he had shared the task force news with her. Together, they had reminisced about the early days with their new born baby, cherishing the memories.

Their son, who is in his early twenties and pursuing engineering at a local college, joined Naresh at the breakfast table. There was a comforting familiarity in their eye-to-eye greetings, each subtle change in expression revealing hints of internal conflicts. Naresh, with his trained eye, could read these nuances. A face free from conflict within the conscience looked bright and clear, and he noted these subtle changes in his son's demeanor.

"What's bothering you, my child?" Dad asked, his eyes filled with concern.

"Dad, what's the use of the bike if it's just gathering dust? Let's sell it off," his son proposed. With a voice tinged with measured rebellion, he added, "Even after I promised numerous times to drive carefully, you still don't trust me. It's like your heart is cast in stone."

"Trust is one thing we see breaking every day in our professional lives. My heart truly turned to stone after seeing the sufferings of the Victims. Anyway, you can take the bike for today. Let me see how much you will stand on your commitment. I hope you remember the unsaid."

It was a custom that CI. Naresh had established to have dinner together at 8:00 p.m. With only three members in their nuclear family; he insisted on seeing each other at least twice a day – once at breakfast and again at dinner. Everyone tried to adhere to this tradition. CI. Naresh will call the family if he is stuck at work but compensates later by spending a good time with his son in his room.

CI. Naresh took a moment to polish his spare shoes and adjust his uniform before his wife. As he turned to leave, a happy smile spread across his face. He felt incredibly fortunate to have a partner who was his constant source of happiness and support.

CI. Naresh kickstarted his 350 CC Enfield Bullet service vehicle and whizzed away. Upon reaching the police station, he diligently cleared some files and took stock of each staff member's workload, offering suggestions where needed. While reviewing Veeru's tasks, he suddenly recalled a thread that the DSP's visit had overshadowed.

With nothing pressing between now and 3:00 p.m., Naresh decided to investigate the matter. He ordered hot tea and some snacks and quickly searched his drawer for the USB stick. Relieved to find it undisturbed, he picked it up, pocketed it to be taken home, and downloaded it onto his personal laptop.

While in the office, Naresh decided to view the contents on a bigger screen. He recollected the last photo he had seen and continued from where he left off. The photos, taken with a 32-megapixel camera, became pixelated when zoomed in. Adjusting his glasses, he focused intently, trying to make out the contents. The color of the dairy has also turned pale yellow, suggesting that the content written was at least a decade old.

Image 14112024108 - Page 1: Dated 16th Nov 2014.

The page detailed a website titled "Naalaayak2Laayak.com." CI. Naresh quickly opened his browser and entered the URL, only to be met with a 404 error ^(Figure 1). It was unclear whether the site had never existed or was simply unreachable. He toggled back to the image, seeking more details.

In the center of the page was a sketch of the logo: the numeric TWO cleverly morphing into the form of Lord Ganesha, with the trunk twisted to the Lord's left, representing the "L" in the word Laayak. The punchline read, "2nd chance for a Better Life." This single page captivated Naresh's imagination, prompting him to ponder the deeper intentions behind the image.

"What a genius blend of philosophy and iconography," Naresh mused. "A beautiful way to suggest Ganesha's blessing for a second chance at a better life."

Image 14112024109 - Page 2

"If we can show a better path for one person in a lifetime, our life's purpose is served. If we transform a whole neighbourhood, you are a Saint. If you transform a Nation, you are Mahatma."

This seemed to be the Vision statement, reflecting the aspiration to guide people towards better lives, thereby building a society rooted in righteous values and ultimately a vibrant nation.

"What is he transforming?" Naresh mused, slightly amused. "We are all Homo Sapiens already; there aren't any Homo Erectus among us. We have codified laws that govern our lives".

This sort of material was not new to CI. Naresh; similar items had been confiscated in previous raids on hideouts of left-leaning ideological sympathizers. He began forming an initial impression of the creator as a potential sympathizer.

It was not uncommon for CI. Naresh to encounter doctors, engineers, economists, and other well-educated individuals swayed by utopian ideologies, dreaming of an idealistic world amidst the chaos. These ideologies often tilted the equilibrium to the left, and law enforcement's job was to bring them back to the center.

"Enough for today; it looks like we need to keep a tab on this doctor. He might help solve some open cases for us," CI. Naresh determined.

Closing the files, securing the open folder, and switching off the monitor, he rose from his seat, adjusted his uniform, picked up his notepad and pen, and walked into the central office space. He saw HC having a heated argument with Veeru. The staff rose from their seats, ready to take instructions. Naresh asked what the matter was.

"His demands are never-ending, Sir. Veeru is asking for the day jobs and, on top of that, he won't be available for the entire next month," explained HC.

Veeru remained silent until CI. Naresh shifted his focus to him, sighing in anticipation of a reply. Veeru explained, "Sir, I haven't been able to complete the portion for my exams, and I'm having very little sleep these days. I've been requesting some flexibility from HC. I can explain my situation to my peers and ensure they won't complain. This is crucial for me to clear the prerequisite qualifications to become eligible for the Police Force exams".

"Disperse," CI. Naresh ordered, and the matter was closed. HC was unsure about the next steps, but Veeru felt reassured of a favorable resolution requiring some patience, knowing the fatherly figure CI. Naresh was in his life and realizing how important education is to rise like a Sphinx.

In the DSP's office

He alerts the driver of the Patrol Van, who swings into action and starts the vehicle. CI. Naresh instructs the driver to take him to DSP's office.

CI. Naresh walked through the aisles of the DSP's office, meeting his peers and saluting seniors along the way. This place always smelled of protocols. While he felt like a king in his police station, the weight of the power ladder he was stuck on became clear here. The only thing he lacked was political maneuverability. Good work can earn a few medals, but other life skills are necessary to reach the top. Still, Naresh was happy because he had time to spend with his wife and son. In contrast, the high-ranking officials often didn't go home for days, mere pawns in the hands of even more powerful forces, such as politicians.

CI Naresh walks into the reception of DSP's office, where he is greeted by a Lady constable. Things have changed a lot. We see diversity in our workplace, which was hitherto a male bastion. The introduction is not necessary, as the name badge speaks for itself. Glancing at my badge, the receptionist directs CI Naresh to the Meeting room "Conan Doyle."

Upon entering, CI. Naresh met two peers, exchanging smiles and checking each other's well-being. They were chitchatting when the DSP entered the room. The IT person was busy adjusting the projector, hinting at a serious discussion. The room, half the size of a boardroom, had six to seven seats.

The sound of boots and the instant snapping to attention filled the air. "Relax, boys. Thanks for coming. I've gathered a few of our best minds today because I want to discuss a case that is overshadowing our reputation as law enforcers," the DSP said.

The DSP carried some newspaper clippings, placed them on the table, and occupied his seat. There were five people in total, with two seats empty. The IT person dimmed the lights, closed the blinds, and started to share some slides.

The team was glued to the screen, listening intently to the DSP as he spoke on each slide:

- Statistics of Missing Persons per Commissionerate
- Open cases of Missing Persons and Average Time to Resolve in Days
- Demographics of the Missing Persons
- Long-Pending Cases of 7 Persons

DSP stated that all the files about the missing persons were centrally placed in a shared folder, with access provided to each CI in the room. The investigation notes, and the contact persons' details were also included in an Excel sheet.

"We have invited two SIs who have done some groundwork to share their findings," DSP said. The SIs entered the room as the IT person opened the door.

The first SI quickly introduced himself. The occupants could only see his silhouette as he stood between the light source and his audience. He started explaining a case featured in one of the previous slides.

"This person went missing in 2016, and the first team that investigated hit a dead-end, forcing the file into cold storage. The file was reopened following a court directive to address gaps in the initial investigation, but it hit a roadblock again. We are the third team to review this case, following the directive to investigate missing cases and identify any related ones that might help solve it. We have followed all the investigative protocols. The subject hails from the bottom strata of society. He was nineteen years old when he went missing, and he will be twenty-five years old today if alive. His father and mother are daily laborers. He was the last and neglected child among five siblings. Though he had no criminal record, he was considered a nuisance in the neighbourhood. Parents lodged missing complaints only after fifteen days, citing unworthiness. They shared a photo of the missing person when he was ten, as none of them had a smartphone. The subject became alcoholic and created drama, much to the dislike of the neighbors. He could not sustain a job for more than a month and did not join his father in working. He only had a basic phone that couldn't be traced as the subscription expired for not renewing the service for three consecutive months. Contacting the relatives yielded negative. The digital footprint has been silent since 2016. There has been no transaction on the Aadhaar since then. His friends include derelicts and drug addicts. Following him, some other cases were solved." he traced the entire case history by the first SI.

The CIs were listening intently. Each had their own set of questions, but they were waiting for their turn. It is the protocol only to speak until their name is called out.

The DSP asked the audience, "Do you want to hear the second case and then open for Q&A, or should we have Q&A on this case before delving into another story?" The audience unanimously agreed to hear the second case before opening for Q&A. Upon hearing the intent, the Second SI introduced herself and started explaining the case details.

"The second subject is a girl in her final year of engineering who went missing in 2019. She belongs to a traditional family with orthodox beliefs. Her father and mother are working professionals in the private sector with good sources of income. She is their eldest child, followed by a brother who is four years younger.

Until her second year of engineering, everything seemed smooth in the family. However, the family noted subtle changes in their daughter that grew over time, creating a rift. She no longer conformed to many aspects of their beliefs, leading to tension among the parents. The subject stopped being bubbly and kept to herself.

The case has been reopened thrice; each time, it led to a dead-end. The girl had a strong digital footprint before 2017, but the activity slowly waned by 2019. Her phone was recovered at home, but it did not reveal any clues. Gold and cash at home were untouched when she went missing. None of her friends went missing, and her long list of friends dwindled by the end of her third year. She did not deviate from the college bus except on the day she vanished into thin air. The last message she sent was to a junior girl who traveled in the same bus, suggesting that she was running late, would come to college alone, and would meet her in the evening. Was this a misleading message? Her parents had to endure the ordeal of identifying unidentified corpses over the years. We also investigated the possibility of honor killing, but there were no hints leading in that direction. Similarly, we explored the angle of 'Love Jihaad' but to no avail. We even sought assistance from Central Teams. We have checked the footage of almost 300 CCTV cameras pertaining to that day. Still, there is no cue". After debriefing, the lady SI stood there to answer questions.

"Please take your seat, young lady," the DSP offered. The IT person took the cue and jumped from his seat to switch on the lights. Unlike the CP's office, there was no automation in the DSP's office.

"Well, these are only two cases you have heard. There are 18 cases of the first type and 26 cases of the second type lingering in our territory, which is just 37.5 square kilometers. If we don't solve these cases, the perpetrators who are on the loose will be credited with a perfect crime. We all know there is no such thing as a perfect crime. Maybe we are missing something and need some fresh thinking. I have classified these cases into two categories: 'Naalaayaks' and 'Naayakins' as our code words. I want to assign each category to one CI to oversee both threads, reporting to me from time to time. You have one month to solve these cases. Any questions?"

Part I: The Caterpillars

Hearing the word 'Naalaayak' for the second time in a day, from two different contexts, sent a surge of adrenaline through CI. Naresh. While it was a common term in their profession, its unexpected appearance in the doctor's vernacular piqued his curiosity.

As the DSP continued speaking, Naresh's mind wandered momentarily, reflecting on his earlier encounter with the doctor. Could there be a connection between the doctor and these missing cases? The doctor's use of the term 'Naalaayak' now seemed less like a coincidence and more like a subtle clue.

Naresh's thoughts were interrupted as the DSP outlined the next steps. Each CI was to oversee one of the two categories, 'Naalaayaks' and 'Naayakins,' and report back regularly. They had just one month to make headway in these cases. The weight of the task ahead settled heavily on Naresh's shoulders, yet he felt a renewed sense of determination. The potential link between the doctor and the case gave him a personal stake in solving the mystery.

As the room buzzed with questions and discussions, Naresh made a mental note to investigate the doctor further. His instincts told him there was more to this story, and he wasn't about to let it slip through his fingers. With the DSP's briefing concluded, Naresh rose from his seat, ready to tackle the challenge head-on, armed with both official protocols and a newfound personal interest in solving the enigma around 'Naalaayak.'

Before leaving, the DSP distributed the work, and CI. Naresh was assigned the 'Naalaayaks' files. The meeting concluded with a ceremonial salute to the superior in the room. After spending some time with his peers, CI. Naresh left for his police station.

It was 6:30 p.m. when he started from the DSP's office. CI. Naresh suggested his driver constable take him through some troubled pockets where the Naalaayaks spent their time. "I want to see these places where they assemble and what they do."

"Sir, this is very early; they usually get active around 10:00 p.m. I can take you at night if you are willing," the driver recommended. CI. Naresh agreed to the idea and directed the driver to head straight to the police station. There, he exchanged his vehicle for his Enfield Bullet and rushed back home to comply with his own rule.

By 8:00 p.m., CI. Naresh's family had gathered around the dining table, which was well organized with cutlery and hot dishes, exuding the aroma of chicken curry and dal. What started as a usual chat, updating each other on the day's events, turned into a lively exchange. CI. Naresh usually kept professional secrets, only mentioning them in very cryptic terms. He had developed the knack of gathering a lot of information while engaging in casual conversation.

"How can the principal act on Sharif and Vikram over a fight that happened outside the premises? He has the right to penalize if the event happened within the college, but what right does he have to act on events that happen outside?" CI. Naresh's son quizzed his dad.

"It has the same implication if you fight, and they come to my home for resolution. My reputation is at stake for events that happen outside the home. Do you get the analogy?" Dad responded, his voice carrying a mix of earnestness and frustration. He hoped his son would understand the weight of his words and see the bigger picture. However, he could see the stubborn rejection in his teen son's eyes, which pained him.

A deep sigh escaped Dad's lips, a silent plea for understanding. "I just want you to know that our actions, no matter where they occur, can have far-reaching consequences," he added, trying to bridge the gap between them. The room fell silent, the air thick with unspoken emotions and the chasm between father and son.

They took nearly forty-five minutes to complete dinner, ensuring every person waited until the last person finished. Care was taken to avoid wastage, and the sound of empty vessels marked the conclusion of an important milestone. After clearing the table, they assembled in the front room and continued their chat.

CI. Naresh's phone rang, flashing the driver's name. He picked up the phone and signalled to speak. "Sir, shall I come at 10:00 p.m.?" the driver asked. CI. Naresh responded affirmatively, suggested everybody in the patrol be in civil dress, and hung up the phone. He informed his wife about the night patrol he intended to supervise. He also mentioned that the next month was going to be quite busy and erratic as he was working on some important tasks.

Findings during a Patrol

CI. Naresh put on a white T-shirt and tracksuit, slipped into his sneakers, and carried his hat. He tucked his service revolver discreetly under the back of his T-shirt. He went to his son's room to bid him goodnight and checked on his wife before leaving the home. He carried a second set of keys to enter quietly if he returned very late.

He was pleasantly greeted by Veeru and another home guard who were assigned night duty and all in civil uniform. CI. Naresh entered the jeep and took the seat adjacent to the driver. "I am assuming that the tip about our rendezvous hasn't leaked? Otherwise, we won't see things happen first-hand," he examined the driver.

"No, Sir, the trip will be a virgin experience," the driver laughed.

"Then show me the virgin Naalaayaks in our territory," Naresh ordered, directing the driver to take him to the places where the unworthy spent their time.

Upon hearing the command, the vehicle, which had been idling until then, started to move. Veeru made a suggestion to the driver, "Shall we start with the arrack shop where the drama unfolds and continues till their homes?"

"Look, the agenda is to observe them, not law enforcement. So, stop at a distance so that the whole area is visible without us being exposed," CI. Naresh suggested. Taking the cue, the driver entered a small by-lane and stopped in a corner, giving the pillion a complete view on his left. The white bonnet of the vehicle was not visible as there wasn't any light around the corner. The neighbourhood was of a lower middle class, comprising families with a myriad of daily struggles.

"That shop makes nearly a lakh and a half every night. It operates till 2 a.m., against the allowed time up to midnight. We get five thousand every night. This is the busiest arrack shop among four others. The owner is a lady don. The kiosks that sell snacks also make a decent buck within two to three hours, and she has a 30% share from those kiosk operators," the driver explained.

CI. Naresh asked Veeru to check on the clientele and their demographics. "But sir, I go for the collections daily. I don't have to pay the cover price to gather this information," Veeru responded.

"You will find people of all ages. There is a hierarchy among them. The seniors are respected, and juniors are given sermons on how to live a life of happiness. Generally, membership starts at around twenty years of age, though there are some teenagers as well, to whom the liquor is given without any verification," Veeru paused to gauge the CI's interest and the dimensions he was keen to know.

"It all starts either as a source of relief for physical or emotional pain and later becomes a habit and then a necessity. Why can't it be nipped in its bud?" CI shares with his team.

"When they have just started, they do not know what they are getting into or assume they can break the addiction at will. Also, what begins as a social obligation soon transforms into a ritual. Why are there arrack shops in this neighborhood and not in the posh localities of the city? It is because the laborers who return from hard days' work get intoxicated as it is some palliative", the driver adds his two cents.

Veeru added some statistics to the conversation, "According to the National Survey on Extent and Pattern of Substance Use in India, nearly **14.6% of the population** aged 10-75 uses alcohol. The prevalence of alcohol dependence is estimated to be around **2.7%**, with an additional **2.5% consuming alcohol in a harmful manner**[1]".

"How is your preparation for the exams going, Veeru?" CI asked with a voice of concern.

"I need a week to prepare for the final year of my degree, sir, but the preparation for the UPSC is falling short greatly. I have decided to work on each thread separately. I need to have this job as well to sustain myself and not depend on parents who are already distressed", Veeru replied earnestly.

When they were engrossed in the recce, a teenage boy was seen approaching the arrack shop. Observing this, CI. Naresh asked the other home guard to intercept the boy and warn him of the dire consequences if he bought the narcotic for his own consumption. "Try to use your power a little cautiously," CI said. Naresh instructed the home guard.

Within seconds of receiving instructions, the home guard jumped into action. He connected to Veeru's phone, which was kept on speakerphone so everyone could hear the conversation. The guard ducked his phone in his shirt pocket and started walking swiftly across the relatively empty road with the pace of a predator zeroing in on its prey. He intercepted the boy just in time, a few yards away from the entrance of the arrack shop.

"Where are you heading? What's your business here? Go away and never come back. Don't you know that you are underage, and it is prohibited to sell liquor to you?" the home guard warned the boy.

Quickly recovering from the intercept, the boy ignored the guard and tried to slip by, only to be obstructed by the guard's hand. Slightly irritated, the boy blurted out, "Who the hell are you to dictate terms to me? Get out of my way, or I'll attract attention. I know many men here. Stay in your remit."

"That's exactly what I'm doing. I have the mandate to uphold the law as the first responder. I can book you under the Narcotics Act and ruin your life. No one can sell liquor to you, and that I can ensure," the home guard spoke with an authoritative tone, assuming it would affect the kid.

Just as the altercation was about to escalate, people started to gather around, eager to take advantage of the drama. CI. Naresh instructed the home guard over the phone to return to avoid exposing their identity. The boy sensed that someone was managing the situation from afar but couldn't locate the police van hidden in the dark alley.

"You go inside the arrack shop and observe from a distance what he transacts," CI said. Naresh suggested.

The boy enters the arrack, goes straight to the counter, places the cash, and picks his order packed in a black polythene cover; he then goes to the snacks kiosk and repeats the same. His hands are stretched, indicating the heavy weight of its content, "For sure, this small fish is going to lead us to a bigger pool," remarked the driver.

CI instructs the driver to follow the boy, keeping a comfortable distance and not losing sight of the subject. He switches the police siren and asks his home guards to clear the two-wheelers parked erratically, obstructing the main road. While the home guards are busy in their jobs, the driver and the CI focus on the boy, who is oblivious to the commotion and shows no remorse.

The boy enters a house where some elders are waiting for its contents. They pounce on the young lad, almost pushing him to the ground. While the elders were engaged in their rituals, disturbing the otherwise peaceful night, the boy was left to his fate. Everything was visible, as these houses lacked boundaries, which often led to altercations among the neighbors. The boy was looking helplessly at the events with wet eyes. CI understood the situation and pitied the boy.

"Let's scout for another story," the CI instructed the driver to take to another location. "Veeru, we need to come back to this house or find a way to talk to this boy in isolation. He clearly needs help", suggesting some daytime assignment to follow the boy.

Veeru acknowledged the task and directed the driver to take them to his home. "You can see one more drama in my neighbourhood. Around this time, we are often woken up by the commotion. I think per capita Naalaayaks are maximum at my place," he remarked.

Veeru guided the driver through the narrow lanes and by-lanes of largely residential colonies of the working class. "Hardworking people with dual incomes from both working partners and medium extended families with strong conservative ideologies live here, isn't it?" CI. Naresh quizzed.

"You are largely right, sir, but the trend is fast shifting. Unemployment, underemployment, and misemployment woes are increasing these days," Veeru responded.

"Misemployment? What are those scenarios?" CI. Naresh asked, curious to understand the new lingo.

"Unemployment can result from a lack of suitable qualifications, a deficit of trust among employers, or a lackadaisical attitude towards work. Underemployment is working in a job that doesn't match the higher skills one possesses due to a lack of opportunities. Misemployment, on the other hand, is using knowledge for the wrong purposes. For example, last week, one youngster was apprehended for using his knowledge in chemistry to create explosive materials from household items and tested it on street dogs at night, much to the dislike of the locals who did not appreciate the utility value of the time of the unemployed youth", Veeru clarified.

The vehicle slowed down just a few hundred meters from Veeru's room, and the team was not disappointed. Just as Veeru mentioned, there was a commotion in the neighborhood. A man in the inebriated condition was the source of the nuisance. "If I knew about this place, I would have avoided it. There are not many options for bachelor men. There's a saying that bachelor men are compared to monkeys sans tails," Veeru exasperated.

Infuriated, CI. Naresh ordered, "Pick up the fellow and throw him in the dungeon. This is enough for today. Leave me at my place, lodge the drunkard in the police station, and then you people break for the night".

Too many coincidences to ignore

The next day staff assembled on time, even though CI. Naresh had very little sleep. His circadian rhythm did not allow him to lie in bed for too long. He reached the office on time as he had to start on the assignment.

CI. Naresh faced a dilemma about where to start, given the two sources of data about Naalaayaks. However, the confusion was resolved by the reply from the Crime Database Administrator (CDA) on the query CI posed a few days ago.

The email provided details on the two photos shared. Both cases were aged yet unresolved missing cases. The email also mentioned that the case files pertaining to the subjects were digitized and available in the archive. Accessing these files required placing a special request to the IT Head, justifying the need to extract and share the data. CI. Naresh chuckled at this joke, as he already had the files he needed in the shared folder. He thanked the CDA for the email and retrieved the photos from the recycle bin to compare them with the cases shared by DSP.

CI. Naresh got a hunch that there was a deep-seated connection between the missing cases and the clinic operating under the guise of a de-addiction center. What was still unclear to CI was the revenue model to sustain the operations. A troubling thought weighed heavily on CI. Naresh's mind: Were these disappearances feeding a sinister downstream illegal organ trade?

CI. Naresh pondered gathering more intelligence before obtaining orders to raid the premises and make arrests, aiming to pre-empt any future untoward events. The unsettling possibility of these disappearances feeding a sinister downstream illegal organ trade weighed heavily on his mind, driving his determination to uncover the truth.

CI. Naresh's train of thought was disturbed by HC, who entered with a casual knock and didn't wait for approval. This only happened when there was some urgency. HC informed him with a concerned expression about the ruckus the drunkard was creating in the lock-up.

CI thanked God for offering him a golden opportunity to receive Dr. Ramesh's services.

"Take the guy to the nearest deaddiction center", CI. Naresh instructed HC without divulging his hidden intentions.

"But sir, we don't keep any database of these services! The protocol is to take the sick to the nearest government hospital or call upon 108".

"Don't bother about the protocol. Let me handle this myself. Parcel that fellow in the Jeep. I am joining you. I know a place where he can get the best treatment," CI. Naresh took the onus upon himself, eager to meet Dr. Ramesh first-hand.

While driving to the de-addiction clinic, CI. Naresh messaged Veeru, "Going to the Clinic, taking the drunkard there," hinting for him not to appear uninvited and risk the cover. CI pretended to have checked the nearest de-addiction center in Google Maps and passed the address to the driver.

Part I: The Caterpillars

The driver placed the siren on the roof, giving them uninterrupted access to the traffic.

They reached the clinic and struggled to take the subject to the 2nd floor. CI. Naresh took the stairs to enter the premises after HC had taken the subject in.

Seeing people in uniform, the receptionist was alerted and inquired about the situation. Sensing the commotion outside, Dr. Ramesh peeped out of his cabin to check. By then, CI. Naresh had also joined the team.

Dr. Ramesh, a clinical psychologist, quickly swung into action, assuming it to be a Medico-Legal case. They took the subject into the cabin and placed him on the couch. The receptionist, a trained assistant, quickly brought out the treatment cart and placed it beside the doctor. Dr. Ramesh checked the blood pressure and pulse, recorded the oxygen levels using an oximeter, checked the pupils, and quickly recognized that the subject had entered the depression stage as the narcotics were waning in his bloodstream.

"Is he in custody? If yes, it becomes obligatory to take him to a government hospital. Not knowing the medical history of a person and drug allergies, it is advisable to treat him in a hospital with all facilities available to handle side effects," Dr. Ramesh explained, exhibiting complete knowledge of trade secret protocols.

"You are right, Doctor. Won't a sedative work to keep him calm?" CI asked to check on the Doctor's knowledge of the pharmacopeia.

"The metabolism of these alcohol dependents is quite different from that of an ordinary person. Each drug reacts differently based on many other parameters. They need to be kept under observation," Dr. Ramesh replied, exhibiting his helplessness in this case. "I can be of help once he's stabilized. By the way, has his family been informed? They need to give consent before we initiate any treatment."

"Oh, I thought de-addiction centers were the first responders for chronic alcoholics. Do you expect people to walk straight into your clinic to get treated?" CI. Naresh quizzed with some added sarcasm.

Unaware of CI. Naresh's questioning methodology, Dr. Ramesh answered professionally, inadvertently giving away valuable clues. CI. Naresh made mental notes of his observations. He noted that a clinical psychologist need not have a medical background and that their approach to treatment often involves psychotherapy and behavioral interventions, focusing on thoughts, feelings, and social factors.

CI. Naresh directed HC to register an FIR, take the drunkard to the Government General Hospital, and inform his family. "They seem to have abandoned this soul," he remarked. He asked the driver to leave, stating that he would make his way to the police station on his own. In truth, he had a hidden objective: to have a long conversation with the doctor, possibly over a courtesy drink in the evening.

With the deck cleared, Dr. Ramesh hosted CI. Naresh, inadvertently giving away more valuable information.

"The office looks very new. Have you moved here recently? You have good taste; I might seek your advice for interiors," CI. Naresh said, aiming to positively connect with Dr. Ramesh's ego and encourage him to open up and divulge more details.

"Yes, I moved here just a few weeks ago from the other part of the city to serve more clientele. I hop between my other clinics and am still establishing myself in this part of the metropolis. Thanks for the compliment; I will convey it to my wife, who helped me set this up. All my clinics have the same appearance as part of the branding," Dr. Ramesh started to reveal more about himself.

"Your wife seems to be an accomplished interior designer," CI. Naresh remarked while observing the room and noting the qualifying certificates that were hung as a custom, proving the doctor's authority on the subject and license to practice.

"No, no, Dr. Praveena is a psychiatrist. We complement each other in our profession. While she provides the medication, I help with behavioral alterations. Together, we strive to give junkies a second chance to lead a better life."

The photo of the logo and punchline flashed in CI. Naresh's mind, connecting the dots and revealing the vision of the couple. "Can we expect realization to mend ever arise in these souls who are in their comfort zone? Will they accept that they are on the wrong side and seek professional help? What's the rate of success, and what proportion of drug addicts are permanently healed?" CI.

Naresh questioned, indirectly probing the revenue model.

"The first step of the treatment is to ensure that they realize the need for professional help. But that step often comes out of coercion. Many times, our clients walk into the clinic on all four legs and go out on two. In India, only about 10-12% of individuals with mental health issues or substance use disorders seek professional help. This low percentage is often due to stigma, lack of awareness, and limited access to professional services[2]".

"Sorry, by legs, you mean physically? Unable to stand like a normal human being?" CI. Naresh asked, trying to understand the analogy.

"Lack of willpower, lack of hope in life, lack of emotional balance, and lack of self-image are what we refer to as the four legs. And two legs mean renewed hope and willpower," Dr. Ramesh elaborates, explaining the deeper meaning.

"We catch these caterpillars and carefully weave them into pupae. After their hibernation, they emerge as beautiful butterflies," the doctor said with a laugh, offering another analogy, which got registered in CI's Subconscious.

"We had introductory courses on psychology in our training curriculum. We understand psychology through game theory, which helps us negotiate with hardcore criminals. Even our department has psychologists, but their energies are drained by processes, procedures, and protocols. They are hardly left with any energy to provide counseling to the police staff, let alone reforming these junkies who don't have anything to offer. At the end of the day, department workers get their paychecks and social benefits from the state treasuries. Their salaries are part of the staff welfare budget," CI. Naresh carefully crafted his question, leading to his quest for details on the economic viability of this trade.

"We choose our customers wisely; we are not Robin Hoods to fleece our rich customers and spend on the poorer ones. The rich customers quickly understand the economic, social, and personal benefits and strike value for money. The poor don't perceive value as the rich ones. Some Samaritans bring them to us and pay on their behalf." The doctor clarifies to some extent but opens another stakeholder in the value chain, and the question lingers in CI's mind, "What can be their interest in reforming these derelicts?".

CI. Naresh understands the need to proceed slowly and always weave an opportunity for future meetings. He senses a connection between the vanishing act and the de-addiction chains. How else could the two databases have common caselets?

The knock on the door gave CI. Naresh a moment to consume the information, process it, and identify gaps to investigate. The receptionist interrupted the flow as she quickly debriefed on the day's tasks before leaving to reach home on time. "I have contacted these clients and informed them of their next visit. I checked whether they were updating their passbooks and reminded them to carry them during their visit. Whenever I had doubts, I asked them to take a photo and post it to WhatsApp.

Only A1021 / 68807 has not picked up the call. I have tried several times and will try again tomorrow."

"So, you refer to your clients with numbers?" Cl. Naresh asked with awe.

"Yes, keeping their identities under wraps is part of our professional etiquette. The receptionist knows the faces of the clients and their codes but cannot map them together," Dr. Ramesh explained, unaware that the trade secrets were already out of the closet.

"Wow, that's quite impressive. I'm having a good time here after a long while. Usually, I'm busy with people and their problems and seldom get to meet knowledgeable individuals from whom I can learn. How are you placed this evening? Why don't we grab coffee and snacks at a nearby café?" Cl. Naresh offered, extending courtesies and friendship beyond professional boundaries.

Realizing that the hospitality for the guest was missed due to an engrossing discussion, the Doctor immediately offered an apology. "Sure, we should be in touch more often as both our professions are common in some sense. While you try to solve the topical symptoms, we try to address the deep-rooted causes". The Doctor unconsciously offered the keys to the door of his heart.

Part I: The Caterpillars

Figure 3: **The Telugu movie from the early 70's that was found among the possessions of Dr.Ramesh**

Figure 2: The MMS image sent by Veeru highlighting the successful completion of recce

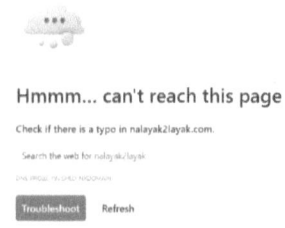

Figure 1: This is the error message CI.Naresh sees when he searched for the naalaayak2laayak.com

Part II: The Pupae

Part II: The Pupae

Foreword

"Naalaayaks" are everywhere and from every social class imaginable. Others give This title when they find the person is in a state without hope of improvement.

These people are like paper kites that have lost the vital anchor thread, drifting in time and space. Philosophically, even if God communicates their purpose in life, they are not in a position to recognize this voice. We cannot term them handicapped, as they are blessed with all faculties yet not being used for the common good. Their family members, friends, and well-wishers have tried all possible reformation methods, starting from advice to corporal, yielding no result.

Much like how butterflies lay hundreds of eggs, hoping at least a few will survive despite their vulnerability, 'Naalaayaks' navigate through life much like caterpillars. They forage time, shedding years without direction or purpose, are vulnerable in their aimlessness, and lack the pursuit needed for transformation.

Just as caterpillars must navigate a perilous journey to become butterflies, these young individuals face numerous challenges and threats. It's a reminder that they need guidance, support, and opportunities to help them transform and reach their full potential. Rather than condemning them with harsh labels, society should focus on providing the necessary resources and mentorship to help them find direction and purpose. It's a complex issue, but with compassion and dedication, positive change is possible.

Part II: The Pupae

Everything Is A Hypothesis

CI. Naresh's visit to the de-addiction clinic cleared some doubts, but not enough to give a clean chit. He understood that the clientele varied across economic strata.

He also weaved several hypotheses that needed validation. One theory was the assumption that if any crime was involved, the doctor couple must be together. Another far-fetched postulate was the possibility that someone in the department might be working in collusion simply because doctors on their own without blessings cannot pull off such a feat. He knows how hard it can become to catch the mole at home; the going cannot be smooth.

While CI. Naresh was framing an alibi to meet the doctor; Veeru entered his cabin in civilian attire. He came to inform CI of his approved absence.

CI. Naresh glared at Veeru, momentarily forgetting his approval of Veeru's casual dress code. Veeru reminded CI of the 21-day absence period starting today. "You have access to the doctor's phone. Should I disturb you for any information?" CI also insisted on transferring the admin rights to the surveillance application to his phone. Veeru dutifully agreed and offered to help in an emergency, noting that some advanced features would require some handholding. He forwarded the examination schedule to CI's WhatsApp and took leave.

"Hope this guy is not eavesdropping on me now," CI thinks to himself. He struggles to locate the application and finally opens the console. There is only one asset that is being tracked. He clicks open on the mobile icon. The application mirrors the phone that is being tracked. With some navigation, CI could locate where the subject is presently on Google Maps. He then checks his calendar to know how busy he is and plans a surprise-laden rendezvous.

To choose the perfect place, CI. Naresh needs to know the common locations the doctor frequents and the duration of his visits. This vital information is available in the application but requires a Pro license, which costs around twelve hundred rupees per month. CI. Naresh finds himself in a dilemma—what he is doing is already out of the standard protocol. The department has a standard operating model for approving eavesdropping, which mandates proof of a crime rather than acting on mere hunches. Even then, the scope is limited.

Ethical hacking can yield limited topical information, but the boundaries are strictly defined. The department does have access to the dark net, which is used for higher purposes such as tracking organized crime and terrorism. However, utilizing these resources for his current investigation without proper authorization could lead to serious repercussions. Knowing that obtaining the Pro license could give him the crucial data required to make significant headway in his investigation, Naresh weighs the risks. But he must tread carefully, balancing his hunches with procedural integrity and the ethical limits of his profession.

CI. Naresh decides to pursue both paths in parallel. He carefully prepares the Surveillance Justification Request form, requesting the digital footprint of movements, calls, and messaging data covering a one-year history and a thirty-day projection into the future. The request includes an AI recording facility to crop the conversations into ten-second teasers based on specific keywords.

This comprehensive approach would provide a wealth of data, potentially revealing patterns and connections that could validate his hypotheses. However, it requires approval and must pass the department's rigorous scrutiny. Naresh knew that obtaining this surveillance data would be a significant step forward, but it also meant navigating the bureaucracy and ethical considerations inherent in such a request.

With the form complete, CI. Naresh submitted it for approval, knowing that he had taken every possible precaution to stay within ethical and procedural boundaries. He felt a surge of determination, convinced he could continue snooping, which could get the official nod in retrospect, covering his digressed footprint.

CI. Naresh summoned HC to fetch the expenses report, as he needed to report on the projections. He had some leeway to alter the expenses to suit his needs. A fund was allocated to oil the 'Khabari' network, which played a crucial role in collecting vital information on the ground. These secret informants were adept at digging to the core of issues and mining a wealth of intelligence. However, this fund was closely monitored to prevent potential misuse, as it could open floodgates if not managed properly.

With the expenses report in hand, CI. Naresh carefully reviewed the projections. He realized that even diverting a few hundred rupees would alert his superior. It wasn't worth the risk of losing his cover. Moving to the next subheading on fuel expenses, he considered alternative options.

These days, the department operates a few fuel stations, and the profits from this enterprise are plowed back, sustainably feeding the fuel requirements of the department. There is a strong directive not to exceed the fuel expenses. Generally, the annual fuel budget is exhausted within nine months each year. While the budget for this heading has stabilized due to relatively stable fuel prices, the increasing fleet size and poor maintenance of older vehicles contribute to higher consumption. This budget is already strained, leaving no scope even for justifiable expenses.

CI. Naresh suddenly had a eureka moment. He identified the Maintenance Head as his savior to fund his purchase of privileged access to the app's information. Without wasting a moment, he opened the app, paid through the payment gateway, and instantly, the subscription was provisioned.

"Hurray!" CI. Naresh exclaimed, overjoyed and overwhelmed at the same time. There was a wealth of information he had to study, which he reserved for the night when everyone else was asleep.

He then surfed through the gallery. The photos revealed some familiar faces. The doctor appeared to be a party man, frequenting popular and familiar bars in the high-end streets of the city. There were many photos with women, but CI. Naresh couldn't place his better half among them. They all seemed comfortable with the doctor, who exuded a playboy nature.

CI. Naresh carefully analyzed the photos, noting potential connections and gathering clues. The doctor's extravagant social life piqued Naresh's curiosity even further. He felt there was more to uncover, and this newfound access to information might be the key to solving the puzzle.

Another important task CI. Naresh recalled was comparing the notes of the common victims from both sources. He remembered that only two photos had been shared with the CDA. Cropping all the photos and sending the mail took him almost eight hours. A task that should have been completed in one hour was extended to eight hours due to numerous distractions.

One significant distraction was a call from CI Ashok Reddy, his peer, who liaised between the DSP and CI. Naresh to coordinate on the thread. The discussion with CI. Ashok, however, did not go well. CI. Naresh seemed to be smothered and left out of the progression list, which only added to his frustration. CI. Ashok is a two-year junior in the Academy whose achievements are less illustrious than CI's. Hinting favoritism at play.

Part II: The Pupae

Unfortunately, in this part of the world, merit often comes second to the tags your names carry.

"What's the progress? Why don't you call in the evening and give an update? I update the DSP daily and expect the same from the team," CI. Ashok spoke commandingly, as if CI. Naresh was his subordinate.

"If there is any progress, I will let you know. Until then, you can mention that there is no progress in your reports," came the blunt reply from CI. Naresh.

"This is not the way to speak to your colleagues. It looks like you could use some training in etiquette. I will recommend your name for the retraining program," CI. Ashok asserted, attempting to emphasize his authority.

"Go ahead and try. Just don't disturb me again. If there is any newsworthy enough to share, you will receive it," Naresh retorted, hanging up the phone to avoid further damage.

CI. Naresh thought for a while and decided to talk to the DSP if it was opportune. These cases are hard nuts to crack, and lateral thinking is a process that takes time. It was a practice in the department to pull an officer down by assigning work yet not allowing sufficient time for outcomes. This was one way to diminish career highlights and hinder progress. Unfortunately, internal politics often favored certain individuals, stifling the growth of others and creating an environment where merit took a backseat to personal connections.

"Oh God, please show me the path and guide me until the perpetrator is nabbed," CI said. Naresh said, seeking divine help and intervention.

While reviewing the register of inmates and the cases yet to be filed, CI. Naresh came across the name of a drunkard who had been admitted to the hospital two days ago. He called HC and enquired about the subject.

"His wife is continuously following up for his release, Sir. She is here. Shall I call her in?" HC informed CI. Naresh.

With an approving nod from CI. Naresh, the wife of the subject was allowed into the cabin. "Please sit down and relax. Don't worry; we are here to help you. Tell me, what is it that you want?" CI. Naresh asked the woman.

"Sir, it is true that my husband is a junkie. He is totally in the grip of banned substances. The drugs have deteriorated his health to the extent that doctors have lost hope, as his liver and kidneys are damaged. He is a guest in this world for only a few more months. My kids and I have indeed endured suffering all these years. What started as weekend parties ultimately consumed him and his family. Please consider my request and leave him without filing any case. Please treat this as a request from your sister", the woman spoke with wet eyes and a pleading tone.

"It is not just your pain that matters when it comes to delivering justice. He has become a public nuisance coupled with several complaints from the neighbourhood. If he knows that the end days are numbered, why doesn't the realization set in and seek repentance? Does he know about his health condition? Share the reports and give the details of the doctor and the clinic you are visiting", CI. Naresh said, not handing her any hope of a quick release.

The lady briskly handed the medical folder to her husband, which she was carrying, and took leave after understanding the next steps. The lady left the Police station without any clarity. She is illiterate in legality and economically strained to bear the expenses of a lawyer to seek bail.

Thankful for the divine blessings so quickly showered upon him, CI. Naresh found an alibi to meet Dr. Ramesh, seeking medical advice on the case. He checked the doctor's whereabouts on the app and discovered him in a remote location. Upon calling, he learned that Dr. Ramesh and his wife were at their farmhouse, about one hundred and fifty kilometers away, near the foothills of a nearby deciduous forest range. The Doctor offered him help on WhatsApp if it was urgent or if he could meet personally tomorrow in the second half. CI. Naresh took the second option and avoided sharing content to retain a clandestine element.

CI. Naresh opened the file to check its contents. He found some reports, prescriptions, and MRI images. As he tried to make sense of the observations noted by the pathologist or radiologist, he came across a crucial detail: 'Atrophy of the left kidney to the extent of twenty percent from the top and inflammation in the right kidney.' This suggested that the problem could indeed be genuine.

This discovery watered down his hypothesis of organ trade, raising the fundamental question about the economic viability of this profession and the reason for the missing individuals. He realized it might be more complicated than a mere organ trade operation.

The basic rule in the investigation was that a person could not be declared dead until proof was found or at least an approver of the crime was identified. Until then, the case would remain categorized as missing. CI. Naresh knew that he had to dig deeper to find the missing pieces of the puzzle and uncover the truth behind the vanishing act and the potential involvement of the de-addiction chains.

He had to wait until tomorrow, giving him time to prepare the direction of his probing. CI. Naresh knew planning his approach carefully would be crucial to uncovering the truth behind the case. He spent the evening organizing his thoughts, reviewing his gathered information, and formulating a strategy to make the most of his meeting with Dr. Ramesh. This meticulous preparation would ensure he was ready to delve deeper into the mystery and piece together the missing links.

"Is this doctor affluent by birth, or did he accumulate wealth in his generation? Is he self-made or born with a silver spoon? Can a psychologist earn so much in their profession? Or are the complementing skills of both husband and wife being milked well?" CI. Naresh's thoughts were all based on the assumption that profits alone motivate humans to do many things.

CI. Naresh realized the dangers of pursuing only one hypothesis. What if it led to a dead end or empty hands? He knew he had to think of alternate theories and put a team to work on multiple threads. Diversifying their efforts would increase the chances of uncovering the truth, no matter how elusive it might seem. By exploring different angles and collaborating with his team, Naresh hoped to piece together the puzzle and unravel the mystery surrounding the case. Apart from money, he understood that people are motivated by various factors such as power, fame, recognition, and self-actualization. "Will tomorrow's rendezvous solve the mystery or add more layers and possibilities?" CI. Naresh contemplated.

His reflection into the future was interrupted by a WhatsApp message from Veeru, 'Poorly performed in my first paper. Preparation wasn't enough. I will fail for sure. I have decided to return to work. At least, I will earn something that will keep me afloat." CI. Naresh felt a sense of guilt for not doing much to give Veeru time for preparation. He knew that if Veeru were given privileges, the other team members would perceive it as bias. It was a delicate balance, and he had to consider the entire team's fairness and morale while supporting Veeru in his struggles.

CI. Naresh called Veeru to check his decision and see if something could be recovered. "How confident are you about the remainder of the courses? If you are confident, continue writing so that only one subject has to be cleared in supplements, which requires less preparation than covering all subjects," he suggested.

"No, Sir, there isn't any support at home. They do not appreciate the effort and hardships I am going through. They only want to reap the fruits of my labor. Their aspirations for a better life do not cross the boundaries of the village. They assume that being away from home means I'm running away from responsibilities. They are unable to visualize the future I want to build for them. They call me 'Naalaayak' and constantly compare me with my brothers who conform to their vision," Veeru almost cried over the phone.

"Your decisions shouldn't be clouded by one exam and the situation at home. Genuinely re-evaluate your preparedness for the other exams. Do this analysis and let me know. If you are not doing well personally, I will ensure you excel professionally", CI. Naresh reassured Veeru, offering support and encouragement.

"In any case, send an email to HC, copying me, cancelling your leave, and confirming that you'll join duties starting tomorrow. The family will not question you if they get their share of honey and allow you to do whatever you want. The contradiction is that they consider your present Home Guard job as the main course, while it is just a distraction in your scheme of things. I will assign you small tasks that you can deliver remotely, and I will approve your attendance. There are budget leaks in the system, and I will defend this," CI. Naresh reassured Veeru.

Veeru agreed to the idea and promised to conclude his decision by the end of the next day. Assures CI. Naresh, he would keep emotions away from his objective analysis.

The crux of the problem

The next day, CI. Naresh called the patrol vehicle driver and reprimanded him for not keeping the vehicle clean and tidy. "Look, I got allergic skin reactions just by sitting in there for one night. How often do you clean the vehicle? When was it last cleaned internally? Bring me the maintenance log," CI. Naresh spoke authoritatively, suspecting there could be more skeletons in the closet than just cleanliness issues.

"Sir, we are allowed a deep cleaning once every six months. We get the vehicle water washed once a week, free of charge, in exchange for some perks. We turn a blind eye to the traffic woes caused by the vehicles parked on the road queued for their turn at the service. Interior cleaning requires shampoo and other consumables, which are chargeable. The alternator is due for replacement in six months, and the central team has yet to procure spares. We are waiting like organ recipients as donors are always scarce," explained the driver.

"You seem to have first-hand experience with organ transplantation by the analogy you alluded to. Is someone waiting in your family?" CI. Naresh asked to know more about the process.

"Yes, Sir. My mother needs a transplant, and looking at the waiting period, she will not get any chance till 2027. There are very few donors," the driver explained.

CI. Naresh further probed, asking if any of the family members, including the driver himself, were willing to donate. "We are hoping that my kidney will pass the tissue compatibility test. I have become a teetotaller for two years to become eligible for organ donation," the driver replied.

The need to check the health data of the missing persons can conclude the hypothesis. The dead-end is appearing to be around the corner.

It was evident that the notes needed to be compared. Until now, the hypothesis had been constructed solely on the coincidental appearance of cases in the databases being compared.

The phone rang, and this time, the doctor called to check if CI. Naresh was coming or if he wanted to reschedule the slot for some other work and meet the next day at the same time. CI. Naresh took the offer, as it gave him some extra time to do extensive research.

With the appointment sorted out, he called Veeru to check on his decision.

"I will continue, sir. I will clear as many subjects as possible so that only a few will remain for supplementary exams. Also, I have sent the mail, Sir. Soon, HC will call and ask me to report. What shall I tell him?" Veeru spoke with a confident tone.

"He will not call. I will handle that. Even if he does call, give some alibi for two days," CI. Naresh reassured him. "In the meantime, check the location of the Doctor yesterday. He has some farmhouse there. Just see where this location is and message me." CI ordered an errand for Veeru.

With things sorted out, CI. Naresh started to read the photos Veeru had gathered. The case sheet revealed that the first subject, Vinay, was 19 years old in 2019 and was diagnosed with obsessive-compulsive disorder (OCD), substance dependence, and bipolar disorder. Vinay had been suffering from these conditions for nearly five years. He came from a middle-class family with both parents working.

The case also detailed the treatment, which took nearly twenty-four months, and Vinay was discharged in December 2021. CI. Naresh noted these dates to be checked against the content in the official folder.

The summary of Vinay's case study suggests that he was cured and is now able to handle the situation better. He received training in the carpentry trade, which was certified by the National Academy of Construction through its franchisee, NL2L Pvt. Ltd Company.

"Wow, what a transformation," CI. Naresh thought internally with a hint of happiness and satisfaction.

He then moved to the next photo of a middle-aged man named Shankar, who hails from a northern state. He was diagnosed with borderline personality disorder (BPD) and was treated between 2019 and 2020. In summary, Shankar acquired the soft skills required to survive while employed in Gulf countries.

These case studies, which appeared grim in the database, were, in reality, a beacon of hope, according to the files. The information from the doctor demonstrated their success in transforming the subjects and helping them live better lives.

"If this is true, are these people victims or victors?" CI. Naresh pondered intently.

To reach a hypothesis, CI. Naresh had to compare the dates with the official files. Interestingly, the dates of the FIR were in a comparable range with the dates of the treatment. Even after considering a fifteen-day delay in filing a missing case, there was still a gap of twenty to thirty days between the FIR and the date of admission. Understanding what happened to these individuals within this gap is the crux of the problem.

What Do You Do With Them?

"Sir, the location is just ten km from my home. Give me your command, and I will gather as much information as possible." Veeru's message lifted CI. Naresh's spirits.

CI. Naresh opened the examination schedule and found that the next exam was three days away. He called Veeru and instructed him to conduct a recce on the farmhouse starting tonight.

CI. Naresh realized that he knew more about Veeru than his own son. He didn't even know how his son was progressing in his studies or what his aspirations were. He reached home quickly after mailing the emergency request for additional maintenance funds and permission to get the patrol vehicle fixed in a local garage.

Not waiting for approval, CI. Naresh drove the patrol vehicle to a local garage, only to find Dr. Ramesh there getting his Toyota Hilux Truck cleaned up, possibly from some off-track driving. They exchanged greetings, had some unrelated chat, and agreed to meet the next day at a designated time.

Veeru prepared for the recce, carefully evaluating the conditions. The days were getting shorter as the hibernal solstice approached, and darkness settled in earlier. During this period, creatures that usually stay close to the ground, like snakes and large lizards, tended to rest in their warm burrows, avoiding the colder lithosphere. This made it ideal for conducting a recce in the fields with shrubs and grass. Additionally, the grass would remain green and not make the noise of crushing boots, providing a quiet and stealthy approach. He stuffed clothing to keep him warm from tip to toe.

With the approach completely memorized to the last twist and turn, not requiring any offline help, Veeru stuffed his bag with the necessary paraphernalia. He also picked some snacks that wouldn't make noise while chewing and could melt in the mouth, providing instant energy, such as 'Parle G' biscuits and 'Éclair' chocolates. He then vanished into the dark, unnoticed by anyone. He also prepared an alibi in case he encountered any familiar face.

After cycling about eight km, Veeru hid the cycle and began walking to the designated place. The path was hardly well-trodden, with the nearest settlement almost five km behind and bordering a forest area. The path also had a gradual incline, and the ground resembled a dumping yard for topsoil from nearby limestone mining pits.

After ascending about four hundred fifty feet, Veeru reached the top of the mound, a tabletop with some stones neatly arranged with remnants of a bonfire. He observed in all directions for any observable light indicating any settlement. Looking back in the direction he came from, the lights were too far away. Similarly, he could see faint lights in other directions. He then looked below toward the direction he had to move and found some well-organized lights and a well-lit building in the center of a large campus. His mobile is showing a dwindling signal strength already. He understood that the signal would not reach the other side of the mound.

Veeru snapped some pictures of the estate from the tabletop, revealing no detail except the lights. He then climbed down the mound along the same rugged path. "Only 4X4 vehicles would survive this terrain; delicate vehicles wouldn't last one trip," he thought to himself.

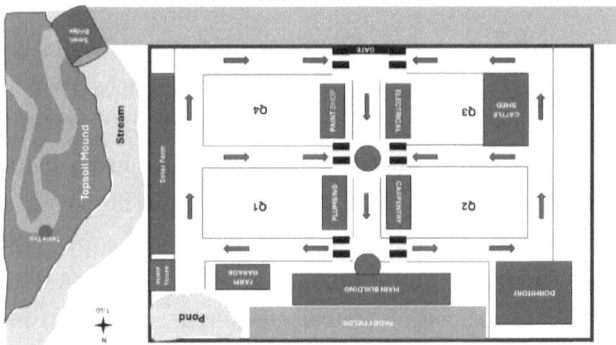

During his descent, Veeru heard voices speaking. Judging that more than one person might be advancing toward him, he quickly took cover behind a shrub. Two men in security uniforms, carrying a walkie-talkie, indicated their position on the outer perimeter well into the mound.

Once the two men were out of sight, Veeru carefully emerged from the shrub and proceeded towards the estate. He reached the end of the mound's downward slope, which bordered a small stream about five meters wide. He took the path through the knee-deep stream of clean water to the right side of a small bridge, avoiding detection at the single-entry point.

Part II: The Pupae

The estate lay hidden from plain sight behind a mound of topsoil debris that had risen high. Vegetation had claimed the land with shrubs and trees of the local habitat. There was only one entrance to reach the estate. After meandering down the slope along the northern side of the mound, Veeru encountered a small freshwater stream with raised banks, suggesting the peak water level during rainy days could reach as high as eight to ten feet. At this time of year, the stream had only knee-deep water.

To cross the stream and enter the other end where the estate lay, a small bridge had been constructed with a fifteen-foot concrete rim pipe. The rough path ended a few meters before approaching the bridge. From there, the road was proper. Vehicles had to slow down while approaching the bridge; otherwise, they could experience a wild jump that could quickly go out of control. This intelligent security feature ensured that anyone unfamiliar with the terrain would pick up speed on the descent, only to be jolted off into the air. The vehicle has to cross the bridge at less than 10 KM speed.

The estate lay on the right after crossing the bridge. It started at the southwest corner, with the southern wall facing the northern slopes of the mound, separated by the same stream. This section was not well-lit. The western wall of the estate hosted the main gate—a well-laid thirty-foot road led into the dark. A small shrub forest bordered the road on the left as if ready to reclaim the land that was once a forest. The road wasn't asphalted but was motorable at good speed. The western wall ran slightly more than half a kilometer.

The west wall is a 7-foot concrete wall, further extended by a 2-foot solar fence. "Is this some kind of Guantanamo Bay? What threat does the owner perceive for such elaborate security?" he thought to himself, marveling at the security measures in place.

After walking approximately two hundred meters, Veeru found a wide gate with an arch that read, "Welcome to NL2L, your 2nd chance for a better life." The logo, resembling Lord Ganesha, was prominently displayed on top of the arch under focus lights. The main gate was also well guarded, with a heavy gate that seemed to open by sliding to the left. A small window on the gate is used to peek out and check on the guest. Fixed CCTVs are strategically placed to give a 270-degree view of the pan. There are no watchtowers.

Taking photos was second nature to Veeru, and he never missed an opportunity to click. He specialized in taking photos directly on WhatsApp, ensuring they were delivered to CI. Naresh as soon as a stable connection was established. WhatsApp, which he uses during clandestine operations, is secured in a folder that is out of sight.

He assessed the estate's size to be around one hundred and fifty acres and fully secure, at least in the front. After reaching the other end of the wall, he takes to the right and sees the wall spread to

the extent he can see. The only way he can infiltrate this complex security is by luring a mole or by getting caught in the act of breaking in; then, the security will take him as their captive. Veeru evaluated the risks but settled with the riskier option.

Veeru continued his cautious approach along the boundary wall, his senses heightened by the anticipation of what lay ahead. Suddenly, a beam of light swept across the ground, illuminating his figure. Veeru understands his cover is revealed by design and decides to run in the open towards the bridge. The two men approached him from the mound and two from behind, their walkie-talkies crackling with urgent chatter.

"Stop right there!" one of them commanded, while the others grabbed Veeru's arm, pulling him to his feet.

Realizing his cover was blown on purpose, Veeru started to play along, enacting resistance by wriggling and trying to slip from the guards' muscular grip. The guards quickly confiscated his shoulder bag and picked up his mobile, hoping to gather information about the intruder. They didn't blindfold him, allowing Veeru to take in the details of the complex as they escorted him through the main gate.

Veeru was taken on a bike, buffered between the driver and a pillion guard. Just before alighting the bike, he noticed the number on the milometer reading three in the red digit. Passing the arch that read "Welcome to NL2L, your 2nd chance for a better life," Veeru noted the well-maintained grounds, lit by strategically placed lights. The logo of Lord Ganesha glowed brightly, casting a serene aura over the entrance.

The inner roads were also not asphalted but well-maintained. Fields flanked either side of the main road, adding a sense of tranquillity to the otherwise secure and guarded estate. Veeru took mental notes of every detail, knowing that this information could be crucial for CI. Naresh's investigation.

Veeru observed several buildings, each with a specific purpose. The main building, well-lit and quiet at this hour, seemed to be the administrative center. He saw dormitory-like structures, training facilities, and open areas.

The path they followed was flanked by lush greenery and well-manicured lawns. Veeru noticed surveillance cameras discreetly positioned along the route, ensuring no corner went unmonitored. The estate appeared meticulously planned, blending modern architecture and natural elements.

The guards led Veeru past a series of workshops and training rooms. Eventually, they reached a more secluded area. The ambiance changed, becoming darker and more foreboding. Veeru's heart pounded as they approached a heavily fortified building, partially hidden from view. The entrance was guarded by a pair of imposing doors, secured with multiple layers of security.

Inside, the air was cooler and carried a sense of isolation. The guards led Veeru through a dimly lit corridor, the walls echoing with their footsteps. They descended a flight of stairs, the environment growing increasingly ominous. Veeru could hear distant sounds, perhaps from other captives, adding to the tension.

Finally, they reached the dungeon—a stark, cold chamber with minimal lighting. The guards pushed

Part II: The Pupae

Veeru inside and locked the door behind him. Despite the situation, Veeru remained focused, mentally noting every detail he had observed on his way in. He knew CI. Naresh would need this information to complete the puzzle and plan their next move.

Veeru knew to keep quiet and composed even in tough situations. He used the time to understand where he was lodged on the campus. As the red digit on the milometer turned to one, the distance from the main gate was almost eight hundred meters. Considering the estate was roughly one hundred and fifty acres, he assumed the building must be bordering the eastern edge of the farmland.

He observed that, contrary to the imposing security infrastructure, the guards were unarmed. The highest weapon they bore was a bamboo stick. Veeru noted this, realizing that the estate relied more on its strategic layout and surveillance than on armed security personnel. There are no sirens and flashlight systems that were usually seen guarding a prison.

Veeru spent almost four hours in the dungeon and slowly drifted into sleep, which was interrupted by the sound of the door. A guard accompanied a lady in her early fifties. The guard switched on the light, pulled Veeru, and placed him on a chair across the table.

"Prathima Ma'am, this is the person who was roaming outside suspiciously around 1:00 a.m. We picked and locked him here. Didn't want to disturb you until daybreak," the guard explained, giving details of the captive.

The lady did not take the chair; she walked towards Veeru and started speaking near his ear, "Hello, young man. I am Prathima, the head of this farmhouse you were trying to break into last night," the warden introduced herself. With no reply coming from Veeru, she continued, "It is basic etiquette to introduce oneself when meeting for the first time. Looks like you are not trained in good manners." She held Veeru's cheek and quizzed while pinching, "What's your name, and what is your business here?" Prathima interrogated. Veeru remained defiant and did not utter a word.

"Get me his belongings," she commanded the guards. They emptied the contents and placed the mobile on the table. The warden picked up the phone and took Veeru's right hand. Her soft-spoken demeanor contrasted sharply with her firm interrogation technique. "Never mind, your mobile will reveal everything if your mouth doesn't spill. Let's try to open the device with your right thumb, assuming you are not a leftie," she said while pulling his thumb onto the mobile screen. Veeru's resistance was broken by the muscular hand of the guard who pinned him to the table with another hand strangulating the neck.

Access was granted, allowing the warden to view all the content. She immediately opened the settings, added her fingerprint, deactivated the hotkeys, and temporarily deactivated the SIM so that the phone could not be traced even by accident.

"Hmm, where should we start? With WhatsApp, contacts, or messages?" the warden mused aloud as she began to surf the gallery instead. Veeru watched in trepidation as she lightly hummed an old song, her cold demeanor contrasting with the casual swiping of the gallery photos. Sweat began to form on Veeru's forehead.

"Ah, this building looks familiar. Let me recollect... Oh yes, this is Dr. Ramesh's clinic. What are you doing there?" she asked, her tone inquisitive. Veeru instantly understood that his cover was blown due to his lack of caution. "Luckily, I removed the photos taken during the assignment. How did this one remain?" he thought anxiously. This lady seemed to know a lot about mobiles. "I only pray to God that the Secure folder is not within her reach," he whimpered inwardly. There was no point in exerting energy; the security would simply overwhelm him. The warden took out her phone and clicked images of Veeru. The security guard held his neck firmly to ensure a proper take. Veeru felt a chill run down his spine as the warden's cold appearance contrasted with her meticulous actions.

"The interrogation is over for now. Your mobile is with me, and I will attend to all your calls from here on and convey that all your bones are broken while trying to commit suicide over the cliff. You are safe and will return in one piece after being fully treated. Well, boy, have a peaceful sleep," she said, leaving the room with the guards who closed the door behind them. Veeru strained to listen to the instructions the warden might give the guard.

CI. Naresh's anxiety increased as he had not received a message from Veeru since yesterday. He called the CDA to his cabin and asked him to trace Veeru's number immediately. "I have sent him on a recce, and he must be in real danger. Quickly get me his last coordinates."

CDA responded in a tone that suggested he was trying to buy time, "Sir, you know the procedures. Our internal processes will take a long time...".

For the first time, CI. Naresh expressed irritation, "Use your contacts and goodwill. All I am asking for are coordinates. We are not snooping into his personal data. For God's sake, use your clout and get the details. One of our own family members could be in danger".

With the CDA tasked with the work, CI. Naresh cleared some more paperwork and then attended to his mail. Among the correspondence was a message from the CDA, which strengthened the positive correlation between the disappearances and the de-addiction clinic.

"I will not leave this guy. My senses were never wrong. There is a deep connection here that I cannot leave unresolved," CI. Naresh muttered, his determination and dedication to the case evident in his every word.

Warden Prathima, deviating from her daily routine, reached her office and organized an emergency meeting at 7:15 a.m. with the key members of the institution, including Dr. Ramesh. The meeting was titled "Code Red." They used the 'Riot.im' application for team collaboration, where members treated any notification from this app as an SOS. All other messages were sent through the usual channels.

Within no time, all the members joined the call with their video on. Ensuring that everyone was present and ready, the warden began the debrief.

"Madam, last night we held a captive who was eavesdropping on our estate. He is not a vagabond; he has an image of Dr. Ramesh's clinic on his phone. He is not disclosing anything yet. We haven't administered the harsh techniques, but he may not even survive a degree less than that. I have shared his photos on your WhatsApp." she paused, waiting for the audience's response.

Every member immediately turned to the WhatsApp messaging app and downloaded the photos with a simple refresh. Each member, including Dr. Praveena, responded negatively, unable to recognize the person in the photos.

"Ramesh, come here at once. You must check on this photo!" the institution's chairman yelled at the top of her voice, as her husband, Dr. Ramesh, was not at his seat when the meeting started. Dr. Ramesh pulled his chair next to Dr. Praveen, adjusting his spectacles as he focused on the image.

"What is Abhi doing there? Has anybody called him for plumbing work?" he shouted.

"No, sir, he cannot be a plumber as his toolkit has biscuits and chocolates. I can check with our approved vendors to see if he belongs to their team. Isn't it strange that the same vendor is also servicing your clinic? Isn't this too much of a coincidence?" the warden probed.

"For sure; He is a plumber. Instead, he is leaking our secrets. Now, he gets to work fast as he can lead the police force to the estate. Initiate the 'Operation Tranquility' for seventy-two hours; we will take stock of the situation then and decide the next steps", remarked Dr. Praveen with a sense of urgency weighing in the risk.

The core members of NL2L were immediately informed of the "State of Tranquility" and set in motion actions that are part of the standard operating manual.

The meeting ended, and everyone was expected to adhere to the set communication guidelines, remaining extra vigilant. Dr. Ramesh immediately called his mole in the police force to check on Abhi. When the name didn't ring a bell, the photo did the trick.

"Oh, this guy is just a home guard, sir. What harm can he cause you? He's an ant you can crush with your thumb. He's posted at the police station near your new clinic," said the mole. These words helped Dr. Ramesh connect the dots leading up to CI. Naresh.

Thanking the mole and promising a reward for helping him get to the root, Dr. Ramesh quickly got ready and took the Toyota Hilux instead of a sedan.

Dr. Praveena left for her clinics to perform the procedures while Dr. Ramesh checked the new estate containing crucial information.

The beginning of a fascinating journey

CI. Naresh opened the spying app to check on Dr. Ramesh's whereabouts. He saw a notification on the app that read "Code Red." Intrigued by the language akin to what the comrades use, he did not open the app to avoid alerting them. He then noticed that the doctor was unusually early to the clinic.

The Head Constable looked puzzled when CI Naresh asked for the gear for a combing exercise. The Head Constable fetched the boots and the bulletproof vest. CI Naresh picked up three additional rounds and registered the numbers in the logbook.

CI. Naresh cannot get help from his fraternity until he has infallible evidence. Many times in the past, he had to be in the thick of trouble to close the case. It is not a parody that the erstwhile Indian movies depicted them as the people who enter the plot when the protagonist settles the dust on his own just to demonstrate that the arm of justice is long enough but not quick enough.

Before leaving the station, CI. Naresh called his wife to inform her of a mission he was carrying out and to expect a blackout period. "I have not heard from Veeru for almost two days; I am going in search of him" is the only snippet of information he mentioned to his wife.

He then called both the Head Constable (HC) and the Crime Data Analyst (CDA) to his cabin and instructed them for the next seventy-two hours. He then copied a sixteen-digit serial number on a piece of paper checking into his phone and instructed the CDA to track them using an Apple AirTag®. Fully loaded and ready, CI.

Part II: The Pupae

Naresh left the station on his Bullet, informing the staff that he was working on important tasks. He categorically delivered special instructions to the HC and CDA to be alert and act promptly for any SOS messages. "Track me if you hear an SOS message from me," was his last command to HC and CDA before whizzing away.

Dr. Ramesh had packed every bit of paper back into the cartons Veeru had helped offload a few days ago. As he was about to load them into the truck, CI. Naresh entered the premises.

"You seem to be vanishing. It looks like I am just in time, unlike the police on the silver screen," CI. Naresh said with a hint of pun intended.

"Ah, thank God, I was asking for help and here you send the apt person. I remember our appointment today, and I was actually waiting. I know you will not miss an appointment that can prove very worthy of a service medal," Dr. Ramesh replied, evoking a sense of déjà vu.

"It means you are sure that your clandestine operations under the guise of a de-addiction center are worthy of a hunt. Thanks for making the chase a lot simpler. Let me be your host; why don't we go to your office and chat there," CI. Naresh insisted.

"Sure, let's go to your station and continue our interview there. Be my guest in my car. Your home guard, Veeru, can pick up your vehicle," the doctor offered.

Listening to the name, CI. Naresh realized that the boldness of the doctor's conduct emanated from the confidence of spilling covert operations.

CI. Naresh hesitantly sat as the pillion in the truck while the doctor took the driving seat and revved the vehicle out from the cellar. He drove to the police station and parked it near the gate. With the windows closed and the glasses tinted, they were not visible to people outside.

"Veeru is very young and has a lot of life ahead of him. Your careless actions can prove detrimental to him. My safety alone guarantees his. If you want to meet him and secure his release, I insist we go to my farmhouse," the doctor blackmailed CI. Naresh. "If you care for him as much as your own son," the doctor added.

"That's a good idea. Actually, I am completely prepared for the action. Let's go and get Veeru," CI. Naresh accepted the offer. It was no longer bait, as both CI and the doctor knew each other's intentions. CI. Naresh always put the safety of his team first, even above himself. This approach won him many loyal subordinates. He was favoured by seniors, valued by juniors, and feared by his peers.

"Wow, you like action. Me too. Let's get to my farmhouse then," the doctor said, pulling the gear and hitting the gas to reach top speed very quickly.

"Why are you careless the second time? With so much know-how on how we work, isn't it worth taking my mobile and all?" CI. Naresh questioned, trying to gauge the doctor's amateurishness.

"You are as harmless as a caterpillar. Your gun will not fire a single bullet. Your phone that is in surveillance will not hit an SOS button. That's my personal guarantee," the doctor replied with mind-boggling analogies that left CI. Naresh shocked internally.

"Let me give you some privileges. You are not a hostage, and I am not a kidnapper. We are friends on a trip. So, relax and unwind. I will try to explain everything you want to know. Let's make this trip, which lasts nearly one and a half hours, as memorable as possible. I promise to make this journey as revealing and philosophical as possible," the doctor offered.

"Promises are made only to be broken, and you rush to make two in quick succession. Your promises are firing much faster than my pistol," CI. Naresh replied, his tone laced with a mixture of scepticism and irony.

"There once lived a mother cow who grazed in a nearby forest. One day, a hungry tiger appeared in front of her. Realizing that her end was imminent, the cow requested the tiger to let her go home to feed her young calves and promised to return to be a happy meal. If the cow hadn't fulfilled the promise, the world wouldn't be talking about this morality tale for centuries," the doctor said, recounting a famous fable retold by grandmothers to their grandchildren in India.

"Well, Lord Vishnu warned Lord Shiva not to give boons to the wicked as his slumber is getting disturbed at the end of each yuga, cleaning the mess Lord Shiva is creating," CI. Naresh added a mythological tinge to the conversation.

"Never met a police officer who is so philosophical. Look, you are neither Vishnu nor Shiva. Let's talk like simple mortal beings. Let's connect to our surroundings.

Have you ever wondered why people break promises? Do you think a normal person enters into a contract with an intention to never fulfill?" the doctor questioned, prompting CI. Naresh to think deeply.

"There can be several reasons why people break their promises. The first one might be because they are not aware of their incapability. The second may be that they realize the benefit of fulfilling the promise does not equal the sacrifice. The third can be a lack of seriousness when promises are made." CI. Naresh began to engage with the doctor in a deep discussion about the workings of the human mind.

The doctor observed that the needle on the fuel indicator was half full and could serve the entire entourage. However, since the vehicle was approaching a familiar fuel station nearby, he drove into the station for a refill. Upon seeing the doctor's vehicle, the staff there became attentive and rushed to help as if he were a VIP. The staff greeted the doctor warmly, and he reciprocated with equal warmth. They spoke to the doctor as if he were a protagonist in their lives. CI. Naresh pondered the emotions on their faces. Clearly, these people were sympathizers and sleeper cells for the doctor's organization. Given that his circumstances could only elicit this suspicion, CI was not at fault for assuming so.

The journey continues after an exchange of niceties with the staff there.

"Sorry for the interruption. These people benefitted from our service and were happy to meet me. So, what were we discussing? Oh yes, I remember now—it was about promises, right? Well, my next question is: When did you make your first promise?" the doctor asked, his tone turning serious as he addressed CI. Naresh.

CI. Naresh wasn't irritated or particularly enjoyed the talk. A portion of his mind was preoccupied with thoughts of Veeru's well-being and the torture the poor fellow might be enduring at the hands of these evil people. Despite his concern, he remained attentive. When his prey demonstrated such calmness, how could the predator feel tensed? He wondered. Subconsciously, CI. Naresh replied, "Maybe when my mother was trying to take an oath when I was a kid, either for doing a task or not making a mistake."

"That's a very obvious answer because everyone forgets the promise they made to the divine to lead a fair and pious life before being granted the human form," the doctor said, his eyes locked onto CI. Naresh's. "How much do you agree with this paradigm? And as a follow-up, how and when do you think one recollects the promises made in the heavens?"

"It's an interesting paradigm," CI. Naresh began thoughtfully. "The idea that we promise to live a fair and pious life before being given a human form is profound. While I may not recall such a promise, I can see the value in this belief. It serves as a moral compass, reminding us of our higher purpose and the ideals we should strive for. Whether or not one remembers making that promise, the notion can inspire us to lead more ethical and meaningful lives".

CI. Naresh is slowly getting restless with the barrage of philosophical questions and trying to ease the tension between them. After all, CI considers the Doctor no more than a criminal as he has clinching evidence. If Veeru hadn't been caught in their web by now, some bones must have been broken. He decides to steer the conversation.

"Keep the crap to yourself and tell me about your organ trading business. How rich have you become by harvesting the innocents, yet you speak philosophy? You are a quack and denigrate Baba in one life", CI was trying to incite the Doctor. "I can hold the gun point blank and get Veeru discharged. I am accompanying you to see for myself your empire built on blood".

"As I promised, you will not use a single bullet because you will not face a gun. Even to encounter a person, you hand a gun to the criminal and then take the shots, right?" The doctor is getting on the nerves of the CI.

"Enough, you bas...., I will, and I can use the gun and get away with some cock & bull story," CI. Naresh choked the doctor's neck, causing the vehicle to hit the divider on a six-lane highway at a speed of over a hundred KMPH. The vehicle lifted slightly into the air before being brought back under control with a screeching halt.

Both realized the danger had been averted. They cooled down a bit and checked the truck for damage before resuming their journey.

"You will have all the answers. We are not into any organ trade, nor do we do anything illegal," the doctor replied in a calm tone. "The riches you see have been accumulated over generations. My parents and their parents worked as professionals. Our family reputation has lasted many generations as fair and pious."

"Your words don't match your actions. You take Veeru hostage and then play the victim card. Are you bipolar by birth?" CI. Naresh remarked, unaware that his comment would provoke an unexpected response from the doctor.

"We are very strong. We don't tend to acquire the traits of our patients even after working with them for years because we are driven by passion. By the way, are you aware that it takes a decade for the last traces of nicotine to leave the body after quitting smoking? It takes nearly three years for the liver to gain functional resilience after quitting alcohol. They are called junkies for a reason; their bodies are not worth a dog's, let alone their organs," the doctor retorted.

The doctor steered the vehicle to a roadside eatery. It was 1:00 p.m., and they had covered only a quarter of the distance. The doctor was feeling hungry, aggravated by the tension. Once again, CI. Naresh observed the doctor being accorded a higher pedestal. CI. Naresh was receiving the honor of a guest, as he was accompanied by the guest of honor.

"So, you are disclosing your soft spots and sleeper cells full of your cronies, assuming that I'll get overwhelmed?" CI. Naresh spoke as if he had cracked a joke. The doctor laughed at this dark comedy and replied, "There is a hell of a lot of difference between love and sympathy, affection and affiliation. Respect and love are earned, while sympathy is free. Affection comes without charge, whereas affiliation is an obligation. You will not understand these subtle differences because you are transactional".

"Transactional? What do you mean?" CI. Naresh asked, feeling deeply offended. He had never perceived himself as merely transactional. He was a person loved by his fraternity and family, and he played all his roles in a balanced manner. At least, that was the image he carried of himself.

"Sorry if it hurts you, but you are nothing but transactional. You are focused on the pursuit of a gallantry medal, which will ultimately evade you as you are pursuing it in the wrong direction. Furthermore, you are wasting your time and Veeru's time as well. He is a young person with ambitions to make it big, but he is being utilized for your purposes, which you will wash away with the term 'service'," the doctor said, his words striking a chord with CI. Naresh, who was already reeling under guilt.

After having snacks, the doctor cleared the payment, lightened up, and started the journey again. "We will take about an hour to reach the farmhouse. You are free to choose the entertainment, or we can continue our conversation if you promise me not to be rude with your pistol. You don't have to use force when I am willing to give you all the details without having to flex your muscles," the doctor said, pointing to some standards of decorum.

"Criminals shouldn't expect decency…," CI. Naresh began but was cut short by the doctor's firm statement. "One is not guilty until proven so. Isn't this 101 in your training? Since when have the Three Lions assumed the role of the hidden fourth one? The judiciary serves justice; your job is to prove the crime. What evidence can you present except for some common subjects? I can prove that we are working on the same side as the police, albeit with a different approach. Do you have proof that we have kidnapped anyone?" the doctor questioned, his tone filled with firmness and logic, making CI. Naresh ponders deeply.

"You are going to hand over the evidence to me in the farmhouse," says CI with a smile with dented cheeks.

"The farmhouse is my real economic activity. I don't earn through my clinic; we generate income through innovative ideas you will witness firsthand. Be ready for utter disappointment," the doctor stated.

"How can it be a coincidence that 20% of the long-term missing cases have some connection with your de-addiction center? Is your clinic the Mecca for derelicts?" CI. Naresh countered.

"Even if there happens to be a cent percent match, they are unrelated. Can we find a correlation between your sneezes and the performance of the Sensex?" The doctor's satirical banter only aggravated the tension between them. "We have entered the off-road track. You may have lost touch with this part of the world since you've been posted in urban centers for the last two decades. Hold the rails tight, and never remove your seat belt. You are safer in the car than outside," the doctor warned, navigating the tight curves and bumpy road along the mound.

CI. Naresh started to consume the details of the surroundings while scouting the habitat. "This mound that we are scaling was once flat ground. About three decades ago, the Mines Ministry identified reserves of limestone here. The mining contracting companies had to dump the topsoil in one place so they could mine the limestone, promising to refill the open mine at the end as part of the environmental clearance. In two decades, the mound they created on the lush farmland donated by my grandfather has grown into a shrub forest. Now, the contractor is reneging on the obligation, citing the destruction of the forest. Even the government officials are aligned with him," the doctor gave away a hint on the source of his income.

"The people who gave away their lands for mining lost their farmland, and the compensation money eroded quickly. They lost their livelihood and were forced to become migrant workers in the city, taking up jobs at fuel stations, restaurants, as drivers, and more. My grandfather's foresight was only recently understood; his action saved our land from mining. This mound now serves as a source of respite to the nearby villages and has turned into a small ecosystem visited by many for weekend getaways. All three generations in our family are professionals in various fields. We have three IITians, four doctors, two PhDs, five engineers, and two psychologists in our extended family," the doctor said, observing an emotion of acknowledgment and amazement in CI. Naresh's face.

They reach the tabletop of the mound, where two security guards are on the watch. Seeing the Doctor's vehicle approach, they come to the edge of the pathway to greet them. The Doctor draws the window on his side and reciprocates good wishes.

CI observes the mound has grown into a shrub forest, "How do you manage to reach this place during monsoons", CI asks interested to know if there is any alternate route.

"The farmhouse is disconnected from civilization for almost four months each year, from mid-June until mid-September and sometimes until October. We stock everything for five months. We did not develop a motorable road around the mound; this is the only road to the farmhouse, both in and out," the doctor explained, noticing CI. Naresh's disappointment at the natural shield the mound provided.

A few meters before approaching the bridge, the doctor blew a long, high-decibel horn, perhaps to inform the security at the gate to open, allowing uninterrupted access to the estate. Just as they approached, the gate swung into action and slid open smoothly without making any noise. CI. Naresh observed the gate and the arch, amazed at the impressive wall.

"If you aren't afraid, why do you have such elaborate security? What is the fear you harbor? From whom do you feel the threat?" CI. Naresh asked, echoing the doubt that had also crossed Veeru's mind.

"The security is for the inmates and their wellbeing. This estate has forty residents on average, including the families of my extended family. My cousin Natraj is in charge here but is currently on a tour in Switzerland, attending technical conferences and business meetings. Our resident scientist, Dr. Prathima, oversees the operations when he's not here," the doctor explained.

They entered the farmhouse, driving along well-laid access roads and neatly drawn plots with fruit trees. The doctor drove slowly to avoid raising dust, allowing CI. Naresh to savor the orchard's beauty filled with pomegranates, lemons, mangoes, and Ber. With the windows open, fresh air quickly filled the vehicle with the fragrance of the farmhouse settling in.

"I will take you on a tour of the entire farmhouse and show you some interesting things that happen here," the doctor said, rekindling CI. Naresh's interest, who had come to rescue Veeru and secure the safety of other hostages.

They reached the barracks and office building, where the vehicle came to a standstill. CI. Naresh was the first to jump out of the vehicle. After shutting off the engine, the doctor also exited.

"Welcome to my farmhouse. You and Veeru are the only hostages who are not junkies and have come here of your own will. We offer services to help you realize the real purpose of your life and give you another chance to lead a life serving a larger cause."

"Why do you talk in parables? Can't you simply say 'Welcome'?" CI. Naresh retorted.

The support staff is ordered to pick up the cartons from the truck and put them in the board room. The Doctor leads CI to a room along a long aisle on the right wing of the terrace. The wings are named after some names which do not resemble any popular figures of the nation.

"That's my grandfather. All the names on the aisles are from my family members. We don't exude patriotism everywhere." The doctor feeds the information, trying to solve the puzzle on CI's face.

The room they entered was labeled 'Dr. Prathima, Head of Psychology Department. Dr. Prathima rose from her seat, looking at the figure entering her cabin along with a uniformed guest. She was astonished to see the CI accompanying Dr. Ramesh. Despite her surprise, she managed to hide her discomfort behind a welcoming smile, her eyes demanding Dr. Ramesh a proper introduction.

"He is CI. Naresh, the handler of Abhi alias Veeru. Their cover was busted, and he came here to rescue him and others who we supposedly take hostage," the doctor said with a tinge of satire in his voice.

Dr. Prathima turned towards CI. Naresh with an empathetic expression. "Hope you had enough of his satirical talk along the journey. He can be very irritating and frustrating at times with his paradoxical dialogues and anecdotes. So, what will you have? Something cool or hot?" she offered.

"I will take Veeru first, and everything else will follow. I want to see him first," CI. Naresh demanded firmly.

"Then let's walk to the room where he is lodged," Dr. Prathima replied, leading the CI.

"I need some rest. I will freshen up while you are doing the rounds of the institute. We will meet in the Board Room at 7:00 p.m. Hope three hours will be sufficient for the tour," Dr. Ramesh excused himself, leaving CI. Naresh in the care of Dr. Prathima for some time.

Dr. Prathima led the way, with CI. Naresh a few steps behind. They walked to the central reception area, where stairs ran down into the cellar and up to two stories above.

"This way, please," she directed, pointing towards the cellar. As they descended, she began debriefing CI. Naresh about the captive. "We found Veeru suspiciously moving around our property with the intention to enter around 2 a.m. Our security captured him and put him in a safe place."

At the bottom of the steps, the cellar branched into two aisles similar to the ground floor. The wing on the left was closed off with an iron grill and guarded by a person holding keys. The guard, armed only with a stick, opened the grill door and switched on the lights as Dr. Prathima descended the stairs. CI. Naresh took the lock and the key before entering the aisle, instructing the guard to walk ahead of him to avoid getting locked behind and becoming a hostage. Sunlight didn't reach this part of the building, leaving it dark and moist.

All the rooms were on the left, neatly numbered "Pupa #1 to Pupa #4." After walking past the first three rooms, the team reached the final one, number 4. Dr. Prathima stared at CI. Naresh who reciprocated with a puzzled look. "You have to open the lock as the keys are with you," she reminded him. CI. Naresh handed over the keychain, keeping the lock of the grill door to himself.

"Veeru, are you awake? Your sir, CI. Naresh is here. We are opening the door, so do not attempt to hurt us," Dr. Prathima announced, asking CI. Naresh to speak as well to reassure Veeru.

"Veeru, I am here to get you out of this place. Stay alert," CI. Naresh spoke, signaling the guard to open the door and enter first. Both the Dr. Prathima and CI. Naresh enters in the sequence. "Where is Veeru here? The CI yelled at Dr. Prathima, who was looking into the dark and empty chamber. He holds the guard by the neck and starts to strangulate him. "Leave him; he cannot hear and speak. He is dumb and deaf by birth. Let me handle". The Dr. intervenes in time. She makes some gestures, asking, "Where is the person who was bought last night?" The guard, after adjusting his neck, signals back with a raised index finger. "What is he suggesting with that raised finger?" the CI. asks with frustration bordering anger. "He must have been transferred to the Guest block on the first floor; let's check there," Dr. Prathima cools the CI, dispelling the fears of other meanings for a raised finger.

This time, CI. Naresh led the way out, carefully facing the doors with his back against the wall until they were back on the ground floor. They took the stairs up to the guest room reception. Dr. Prathima opened the register to check the occupants of the guest rooms. "Here he is, allocated to room #103," she said, leading the way to the room, only to find the door locked. The key was not at the reception either. It was clear that Veeru must still be on the campus.

"He must be in the field. It is 3:30 p.m. now, and people usually are in the field until 6:00 p.m. Shall we wait for their return, or should we proceed to the spot ourselves?" Dr. Prathima asked, checking CI. Naresh's preference.

CI. Naresh pulled out his phone to call Veeru instead and observed the signal was weak and inconsistent. If anyone was trying to reach him at this time, they would hear the message: 'out of coverage area.' The wait was becoming spooky for CI. Naresh. "Take me to him," he commanded Dr. Prathima.

"Don't get anxious; he is safe on campus. He will return along with others after the shift ends."

"What shift? He is not your farm laborer," CI. Naresh spoke with harshness in his tone.

"We don't follow the Geneva Conventions in this place. Every soul on campus earns their bread only after exerting some physical activity. The 'No Work - No Food' policy applies even to our guests. From tomorrow, even you will work in the field. If you want to gain first-hand experience of what life here is like, I will take you on a tour, and you can choose the place that interests you," the doctor said.

"You will be the first person to make a laborer out of a police officer," he laughed wildly at the prospect of working to earn bread.

"People from the highest public positions come here and humbly work in the fields. You are not the first, nor will you be the last. We have high court judges, SPs, DSPs, CPs, and doctors as our guests. They usually come here on weekends and have a good time," Dr. Prathima said with confidence.

CI. Naresh remembered that Veeru had to prepare for an exam on Saturday, which was now just forty-eight hours away. Veeru had been stuck here for the past forty-eight hours, likely missing his preparation. He felt a sense of guilt.

"Look, Doctor, my patience is waning. Before I turn violent and do some harm, either take me to Veeru or get him here at once. I want to check on his safety first. You must have walkie-talkies or some other means of communication to reach the dispersed teams. Activate them and check his coordinates. I don't want a negative on the next search," CI. Naresh issued a stern warning.

"Let's get to the boardroom floor. The surveillance set-up is in that room", Dr. Prathima said. They took the central stairs to the topmost floor, which had two wings again. The central reception area of this floor was filled with photos of ordinary-looking people.

"Are these people related to Dr. Ramesh?" CI. Naresh asked, curiosity piqued.

"No, they are our success stories. They are our inspiration. They are our butterflies who have transformed in our care and embraced the second chance to lead a better life. If you happen to visit again next year, you will see photos of those who graduate this year", Dr. Prathima explained.

Dr. Prathima swiped her finger on the digital lock to gain access to the Board Room and entered. The motion detectors activated the lighting. CI. Naresh followed her, taking in the details of the room. It was large, well-furnished, and modern, equipped with a large screen and video conferencing facilities.

While Dr. Prathima got busy switching the screen and changing the input to the CCTV feed from the console in the center of the table, CI. Naresh checked the entire room. He walked around the table and reached the window at the rear end, near the head of the table. Moving the blinds, he saw that the eastern wall was about a hundred meters behind the building, with paddy fields filling the space between the building and the wall.

The feed from about 50 CCTV cameras was available on the list. Dr. Prathima picked up the walkie-talkie set and started surfing some strategic cameras.

"Narayana, come in. Narayana, come in," she said, waiting for a response while the walkie-talkie hissed.

"Yes, Madam, Narayana speaking."

"Is Veeru with you? Our guest who was introduced at the breakfast table?"

"No, Madam, he is not here. I haven't seen him boarding for Quadrant III".

Standing at the corner of the room, CI. Naresh keenly observed the CCTV feed. It appeared that no part of the estate was left out. The feed quality was excellent, with a zoom facility that allowed for close inspection of various areas.

Dr. Prathima thanked Narayana and then contacted the supervisor of Quadrant IV and other supervisors in the sequence. While she was busy, CI. Naresh's eyes caught the feature map of the estate hung on the wall. He approached it to understand the layout better. The estate was well-planned, with plots clearly demarcated for specific purposes. The estate is clearly demarcated into Four Quadrants, with the main building occupying the remaining portion at the end. There were barracks for people, a water harvesting pond, garages for farm equipment, power switchgear equipment, and sheds for dairy animals. This appeared to be a self-sufficient estate. The roads were narrow, necessitating a one-way policy for vehicles within the estate, which was clear with the arrow markings. The arrows on the right side of the main building went clockwise, while those on the left went anti-clockwise. The residential barracks were also well maintained, with lawns in the front and walkways. The gardens made use of the natural slopes.

After completing the conversations with all the supervisors, Dr. Prathima turned to CI. Naresh, who was still studying the map. She drew his attention by saying, "Veeru is not traceable within the farmhouse. It looks like he slipped into the forest, as the northern wall has some weaknesses. He must have figured this out and found his way". Her face showed no signs of anxiety or worry, which only aggravated CI's irritability.

"We must speak to the van driver. Let's quickly get to the dormitories. The van must be returning anytime soon." After this, she instructed all supervisors on Walkie-talkies to assemble at the Dormitory and asked the van driver to stay back, as we all needed to go on a search party tonight.

Dr. Prathima and CI. Naresh made their way towards the dormitories, where the supervisors were expected to return. The sun was beginning to set, casting long shadows across the well-maintained estate. The air was filled with the earthy scent of the fields and the distant hum of activity.

As they walked, CI. Naresh couldn't help but notice the meticulous planning and efficiency of the estate. The narrow roads, the neatly arranged plots, and the strategic placement of buildings all spoke of careful thought and purpose.

They arrived at the dormitories just as the supervisors were returning from the fields. Dr. Prathima called out to them, "We need to check if anyone has seen Veeru. Please gather around".

The supervisors, a mix of seasoned workers and newer recruits, formed a circle. They listened attentively as Dr. Prathima explained the situation. CI. Naresh scanned their faces, looking for any sign of recognition or concern.

CI. Naresh's impatience grew. "We need to find him immediately. He has an important exam to prepare for, and time is running out".

"We will organize a search party and cover every part of the estate," Dr. Prathima assured him. "Let's start with Quadrant IV and then expand our search from there."

After resting, Dr. Ramesh freshened up and moved towards the boardroom, assuming that CI. Naresh and Dr. Prathima would be there. The door of the Board Room was closed, and there was no sign of life inside. Swiping his fingerprint, he gained access to the room. He then took a seat and quickly connected to his email. He picked up his phone, which was connected to the Wi-Fi network using satellite services provided by Airtel, ensuring a stable internet connection. He then picks the Walkie-Talkie to check on each supervisor.

"Shankar, come in. Shankar," he called to one of the supervisors.

"Good evening, Sir. Shankar here. We have formed a search party to scout for Veeru, who is missing. Warden Madam is also with us, and we have someone from the police department. We are about to leave from the dormitory and start from Quadrant IV," the supervisor reported.

"OK, I will also join the search. The CI and I will cover Quadrants II and III, and your team will cover Quadrants I and IV. You people carry one set of radio sets; I am bringing the set from here. Also, take the full beam torch. Keep one set for us," Dr. Ramesh instructed. With that, he rushed to the dormitory where CI. Naresh was waiting.

The CI and Dr. Ramesh were reunited. "I can understand the pain when a person is separated. The memories with that person haunt you, especially if there is some emotional connection," Dr. Ramesh spoke.

"Empty words, Doctor. Those are hollow statements. If you really cared for the families of the victims, you wouldn't kidnap them," CI. Naresh retorted.

"But what if the families were gifted back their loved ones completely transformed? What if the person who went missing returns home a different person, devoid of dependencies and addiction? Would the families still feel the same pain?" Dr. Ramesh tried to reason.

"That is what you do in your clinic back in the city; here, you are doing something completely different," CI. Naresh rejected the claim of reformation happening in the farmhouse.

"You must see to believe it. Let's start from the place where he was held hostage. You might have seen it in the afternoon, but we will see it again in a different light with me," Dr. Prathima insisted, urging a revisit to the dungeon in the cellar of the main block.

The doctor signaled the dumb and deaf guard in the cellar, asking him to open all the rooms. He quickly executed the orders.

"These people are lucky in some ways, as they don't hear the pain of transformation. They cannot hear the sounds of people in agony who are fighting against the depressants. Do you see the rooms here? They are used to treat patients with addictions. Our techniques sometimes border on cruelty, but that's the only way to drive the devil out of a person. These rooms are devoid of any light. In the darkness, the human mind works in different ways. Ultimately, it gives them time to think and reflect. It might take a week or months, depending upon the individual willpower. This is the fear they will remember to avoid in the future. Isn't it similar to your third-degree torture to get to the core of the crime?" the doctor asked.

"We aren't that cruel. Actually, our hands are at times curbed by the Human Rights Activists," CI. Naresh responded.

"Yes, we wanted to avoid those urban activists who claim to be the watchdogs of human rights. Our treatment techniques are not always humane, and we do not like intervention in our process, as it often dilutes the treatment and confuses the patient," Dr. Ramesh reiterated, emphasizing the need to have this facility away from urban centers.

"You still cannot justify the kidnap. Even if the families acquit you, you have crossed the red line by law," CI. Naresh said, trying to explain that the methods used were illegal.

"I understand your perspective, and I don't expect everyone to agree with our methods. But sometimes, the conventional ways fail to make a difference, and we are left to explore alternatives, even if they are seen as radical. The ultimate goal is the transformation and rehabilitation of individuals who have lost their way," Dr. Ramesh responded, trying to convey the complexity and intent behind their actions.

Their discussion was interrupted by the hissing of the walkie-talkie coming to life. "Dr. Ramesh, please come in. We found Veeru. He was trying to scale the north wall and escape into the jungle," Dr. Prathima spoke with a sense of achievement.

"That's good news! We saved a life from becoming dinner to the wild cats. Let's all meet in the mess hall. We will have dinner together and break for the night," Dr. Ramesh commanded.

CI. Naresh and Dr. Ramesh left together for the dormitory, which housed the canteen facility, where food was served for all. It is the place where all the farmhouse occupants meet and have breakfast and dinner together like a family.

"So, there is a long list of accused in this crime. How many people will have to be booked?" the CI regained his sense of humor.

"You will decide on it tomorrow. For now, let's get to the canteen. I am hungry, and you will be happy to meet Veeru."

Part III: The Butterflies

Foreword

Part III: The Butterflies

The "Butterflies" section is dedicated to the remarkable individuals who have embraced transformation and newfound hope through our institution. Each story within these pages is a testament to the resilience, courage, and unwavering spirit of those who chose to rewrite their destinies. As you read their journeys, you will witness the profound impact of compassion, support, and the belief in second chances. These narratives not only inspire but also remind us of the boundless potential within every individual to change and thrive. Welcome to the world of the Butterflies, where hope and transformation take flight.

Part III: The Butterflies

Seeing Through The Lens Of Others?

This time, CI. Naresh was walking ahead, feeling confident and more comfortable about the premises. His impression of the farmhouse and Dr. Ramesh started to appear in a better light. He began to acknowledge the good work Dr. Ramesh was doing, albeit a little grey in scale. Respect for Dr. Ramesh began to set in some corner of his heart. However, he still wanted to ensure that Veeru was not subjected to any harsh treatment.

As they reached the mess hall, the warm, communal atmosphere was apparent. People were gathering, chatting, and preparing for dinner. The aroma of food filled the air, adding to the sense of camaraderie.

Dr. Prathima approached them with a relieved smile. "Veeru is fine. He is a bit shaken but unharmed. He's in the infirmary right now, getting checked by our medical team."

CI. Naresh nodded, relieved to hear this news. "I'd like to see him, to make sure he's really alright."

"Of course," Dr. Ramesh replied. "I'll take you there myself."

They made their way to the infirmary, where Veeru was sitting on a bed, looking tired but otherwise okay. The medical staff were wrapping up their examination.

"Veeru," CI. Naresh said gently, "are you alright?"

Veeru looked up and nodded. "Yes, sir. I'm fine. Just a bit tired and scared. But they treated me well. No one hurt me."

The CI felt a wave of relief wash over him. "That's good to hear. We'll make sure you're prepared for your exam."

Dr. Ramesh spoke up. "Veeru can rest here tonight. We'll ensure he's comfortable and gets everything he needs."

With Veeru's well-being confirmed, they headed back to the mess hall for dinner, the tension finally easing.

Veeru tagged along closely with CI. Naresh, not leaving even his shadow. The members of the search party lit up the atmosphere in the Mess Hall. Each member came along and introduced themselves, creating a warm and welcoming environment.

Dr. Ramesh, rising from his bench, announced to all that an "all-hands meeting" would be held tomorrow under the auspices of the chief guest, CI. Naresh. "Gentlemen and Prathima Madam, let me take the privilege of introducing our guests to the larger team here. You were introduced to this cat already this morning," Dr. Ramesh said, placing his hand on Veeru's shoulder. "Now we have the father cat who came here to rescue him, assuming the baby cat is in danger. The father cat is none other than CI. Naresh. They are our state guests who will receive the highest protocol.

We will have a different setup here tomorrow, one that resembles a courtroom. The officer in charge will review our activities, and we request full cooperation from all the butterflies here. So, please help in making the setup tonight. We will also have other guests who will join us in the evening, and we shall have good entertainment on campus," said Dr. Ramesh, raising his toast.

CI. Naresh reciprocated the gesture, and the room echoed with anticipation and readiness for the upcoming day.

After dinner, Dr. Prathima handed over the keys to the suite on the third floor of the main building. After a satisfying meal, the team slowly strolled towards their respective rooms.

Veeru opened the door and entered first. Once he signaled that the room was clear, CI. Naresh entered and closed the door behind them.

"Can you check if we are bugged?" the CI asked Veeru.

"I can't say for sure, sir; they are really high-tech. Anyway, allow me to take a look." Veeru got into action, searching for hidden cameras and microphones. The room was devoid of decorative items that could be used as obvious camouflage. Veeru took his mobile phone, switched on the torchlight, and used it to inspect the only mirror, checking if it was layered.

Part III: The Butterflies

After spending about ten minutes thoroughly searching the room, Veeru confirmed that it wasn't bugged but advised them to talk quietly.

The CI. asked Veeru to come close and started speaking very softly, "Now tell me everything. How did you land here? How were you treated after being caught? Did you".

"Sir, I was caught between 3 and 4 a.m. It was by design, as I did not find any gaps in the security of the fortress. I made myself appear suspicious so that they would take me in. The first element of surprise is that they are unarmed inside. Their only offense is the best defense. I was taken into the cellar of the main building, not blindfolded. I was lodged in the dungeon for about four hours before Warden Madam visited. That encounter was terrifying. It was the first time I felt fear in my spine. She got all the information with ease, without straining any muscle. After about an hour, I was taken to the second floor and offered room #103. They provided me with toiletries since I hadn't planned for them. I was asked to assemble in the dormitory for breakfast. I was on my own. I went to the dormitory as I was hungry. There, I was introduced to the four supervisors. Later, Dr. Prathima offered me the choice of either resting or roaming freely on campus. I chose the latter as I wanted to check out the campus," Veeru paused, sensing that CI. Naresh had many questions.

"Didn't they hurt you?" the CI asked, surprised.

"No, sir. The maximum atrocity they showed was lodging me in that dark room for 4 to 5 hours. After that,

Part III: The Butterflies

I had full freedom to roam the campus. The campus is a beautiful place with orchards, paddy fields, and sheds with different trades. The people were very hospitable and happy. There were people learning different trades, such as carpentry, plumbing, and electrical work. There weren't many in each class, so the supervisors were giving their full attention to each member. The fields are highly mechanized, requiring very little labor. I rested under some trees when I got exhausted," Veeru explained the workings of the farmhouse.

"Then why did you try to escape?" the CI asked.

"I wanted to contact you. For that, I had to scale the mound and reach the tabletop, the only place where the signal was reachable," Veeru replied.

"Did you get any clue on how these people here have arrived? Like details of their kidnap, etc?", the CI. Naresh queried.

"No, Sir. I did not speak to anybody on this subject. But one thing is strange here: They refer to them as Butterflies and with some number," replied Veeru.

"Interesting," CI. Naresh mused. "So they dehumanize them by stripping away their names and identities, reducing them to numbers. That's quite unsettling."

Veeru nodded. "Yes, sir. They're trying to erase and replace who they were with something new. The term 'Butterflies' might signify their transformation process, but it still feels wrong."

CI. Naresh leaned back, deep in thought. "We need to understand their methods and what happens during these transformations. Tomorrow's meeting will be crucial."

Veeru agreed. "Yes, sir. We should be prepared for anything."

As they settled in for the night, both men knew that the coming days would be challenging and that they needed to stay vigilant to uncover the truth about the farmhouse and its mysterious operations.

Part III: The Butterflies

Courtroom interrogation

The CI and Veeru got ready and walked towards the dormitories. Today, breakfast was being served in the open. Dr. Ramesh, Dr. Prathima, and another lady were waiting for the guests.

Dr. Ramesh quickly introduced the lady, "This is Dr. Praveena, my wife and a trained psychiatrist."

While savoring the breakfast, Dr. Ramesh spoke, "I hope you caught some sleep. Rest is very important for recovery. Today, you are going to judge us on our work. You are free to investigate, and we will offer our full cooperation."

CI. Naresh nodded, appreciating the openness. "Thank you, Dr. Ramesh. We will conduct our investigation thoroughly and fairly."

Dr. Prathima chimed in, "We believe in the work we are doing here and are confident that you will see its value."

The atmosphere was charged with a mix of anticipation and readiness as everyone prepared for the day ahead.

A supervisor walked up to CI. Naresh and offered him the robe of a judge. The CI was surprised to see the robe of a judge in this place. "Sorry, I cannot wear this as protocol prohibits," CI said. Naresh said, denying the offer. Instead, he picked up the robe and handed it to Veeru. "You wear it. Be careful of any bias. I am not your boss for today. I will play the role of a public prosecutor on behalf of the victims."

"Are you sure? Is he the right person to judge?" Dr. Ramesh asked.

"Yes, Veeru is not biased. He has also turned twenty-one and hails from the same demographic as the victims, so he can connect with the case. He is emotionally balanced, aware of social problems, and has the capacity for original thought. Let him judge the case at hand. I will try to punch holes in your method and make you feel guilty. This will make my process easier," CI. Naresh reiterated.

Dr. Ramesh nodded, accepting the arrangement. "Very well. Let us proceed."

Veeru donned the robe, feeling the weight of the responsibility it symbolized. The atmosphere grew more serious as the others watched the interaction.

The makeshift courtroom buzzed with anticipation as everyone took their places, ready to begin the proceedings that would shed light on the methods and ethics of the farmhouse operations.

Opening Scene:

"My Lord, today we have victims amongst us who were uprooted from their families by force and have been lodged here. Their families have lost all hope of their return. The police machinery also lost traces of these people in the investigation. Here, their identities are stripped, and they are referred to with mere numbers. I would seek your permission to speak to some of these victims," CI. Naresh initiated the proceedings.

"Permission granted," Judge Veeru allowed.

One of the supervisors called out, "Butterfly 101, Butterfly 101."

The victim, Butterfly 101, entered the witness box, took the oath, and stood attentively to answer the barrage of questions from the public prosecutor.

"So, Butterfly 101, what is this strange name you have? Is this the name given by your parents? Tell us everything about yourself and how you ended up here. Tell the judge how you were treated here and the torture you were subjected to," CI. Naresh asked the first victim.

"I am one among many butterflies here. We all share similar stories. I can speak on behalf of all the butterflies here today and the alumni. Our parents might have given us names, but those names bring back bad memories in our lives. We had gone through some rough patches in our early years. We drifted afar; we did not have an anchor. Parents, siblings, life partners—all have been a source of discomfort. We were blaming the outside world, all the while not knowing the pain we caused them. Here, we are given different names, we are coached to realize our vices, and we are trained to live a fulfilled life. So even if my name is odd, I don't care because I will be remembered by what I do for society after getting released from this pupae stage," Butterfly 101 explained.

The CI. Naresh was handed the case booklet pertaining to Butterfly 101 by a supervisor. Quickly flipping through the file, he read some of the content aloud.

"So, your real name is Chandrasekhar, alias Chandu. You are from the southeastern part of the city. You were lodged here on the 23rd of February 2024, and it has been almost 10 months since you were brought here. Can you tell the judge how you were brought here? Under what circumstances were you taken hostage?" CI. Naresh questioned the witness.

Butterfly 101, or Chandu, took a deep breath before answering. "It was a difficult time for me. I was heavily into substance abuse and had lost control over my life. One night, I was wandering the streets in a stupor when a van approached me. I don't remember much, but I was forcefully taken inside. When I woke up, I was in this facility. At first, I was terrified and angry. I didn't understand why I was here or what was happening. But over time, I started to see the changes in myself and others around me".

He paused, gathering his thoughts. "They treated me with a strange mix of kindness and strictness. It wasn't easy, but I started to understand the purpose behind their methods. They wanted to help us break free from our past and build a better future. The initial experience was harsh, but it paved the way for my recovery".

CI. Naresh listened intently, noting the mixed emotions in Chandu's account. "So, you're saying that despite the forceful way you were brought here, you believe the treatment helped you?"

Chandu nodded. "Yes, sir. It's not something I would have chosen for myself, but in hindsight, it saved my life".

"Please note this, your honor: the person was not picked by choice but by force," CI. Naresh emphasized. Turning towards the witness, he continued, "It might have helped you, but the method deployed cannot be considered legal by any standards. Anyways, please elaborate on the torture you were subjected to on these premises."

Butterfly 101, or Chandu, took a deep breath before responding. "When I first arrived, I was placed in a dark, small room for several hours. It was terrifying and disorienting. The lack of light and the isolation made it feel like an eternity. They called it the 'pupae stage,' where we were supposed to reflect on our past actions and the pain we caused to others."

He paused, gathering his thoughts. "The psychological pressure was immense. They used various techniques to break us down mentally and emotionally. We were constantly reminded of our past mistakes and the harm we had done. It was a form of mental torture, but they believed it was necessary for our transformation."

Chandu looked around the room, his eyes reflecting the pain of his experiences. "There were times when I thought I couldn't take it anymore, but eventually, I started to see the changes in myself. The process was harsh, but it forced me to confront my demons and work towards becoming a better person."

CI. Naresh listened intently, noting the mixed emotions in Chandu's account. "So, you're saying that despite the forceful way you were brought here and the harsh methods used, you believe the treatment helped you?"

Chandu nodded. "Yes, sir. I am saying this without pressure or coercion from anyone. I am sure many of my fellow butterflies share the same emotions," Chandu said, glancing at the benches where his peers were seated.

CI. Naresh took a moment to absorb Chandu's words. "Thank you for your honesty, Chandu. Your testimony is important."

Turning to the judge, CI. Naresh continued, "Your honor, while the positive outcomes are acknowledged, the methods used to bring these individuals here and the initial treatment they received raise serious ethical and legal concerns. We must ensure that any form of rehabilitation respects the rights and dignity of individuals."

Judge Veeru nodded thoughtfully. "I understand the complexities involved. We will continue to hear from other witnesses to get a comprehensive understanding of the situation. You may ask any other questions relating to his profession, his family, and the problems he created in his previous setup".

"Objection, my lord," Dr. Ramesh stood up, objecting to the judge's suggestion. "Discussing past traumas can reopen old wounds from which the witnesses are trying to recover. We request the public prosecutor to be careful in his interrogation, as it could hamper their recovery and potentially dilute the progress achieved so far".

The atmosphere in the makeshift courtroom was tense yet hopeful as everyone awaited the next steps in the proceedings.

"Objection sustained. Mr. Public prosecutor, you should be careful in your questioning and respect the boundaries as suggested by the defendant", judge Veeru pointed out.

"Thanks, your honor. I will take cognizance of the matter." Turning again to the witness, the CI starts his questioning.

"Didn't you yearn to connect with your loved ones in the past ten months? Do you have any idea of the trauma they must be undergoing? Why are you so harsh on them?" the public prosecutor probed.

"Our loved ones are always in our thoughts. We understand that time heals pain; by now, they must have settled into life without us. The only pain they might carry is the unresolved outcome of their police complaint. Depending on the hurt we caused them, they might have accepted our non-traceability as a form of death. We have drifted so far in our relationships that we have become inconsequential to them. Their lives might be better off without our constant presence and pestering, but it doesn't erase the ache in our hearts. Despite everything, we still miss them and hope that one day, we can make amends".

"Thanks, Butterfly 101, you may leave now. We will call you again if necessary, so don't leave the court," CI. Naresh dismissed the witness and turned to the judge. "Your honor, I would like to interrogate Dr. Prathima, and I request your permission."

As soon as the judge granted permission, the supervisor called out, "Dr. Prathima, Dr. Prathima." After administering the oath, the channel for interrogation was opened to the public prosecutor.

"So, you are Dr. Prathima. Where did you complete your M.B.B.S? What is your role here?" the public prosecutor started.

Turning towards the judge, Dr. Prathima spoke, "Your honor, I am a Doctor of Horticultural Sciences. I am the Warden of this farmhouse. As a warden, I am responsible for the safety and welfare of all living beings on the campus, including orchards and livestock. I am tasked with taking any action that ensures the safety of the residents," she explained.

"That's a tall responsibility, one which you seem to neglect," the public prosecutor remarked.

"Objection, my Lord," Dr. Ramesh interjected. "The public prosecutor must remember that his role is to present evidence of any misconduct by the witness, not to pass judgment. Delivering a verdict is the sole prerogative of this court. I request that he refrain from making such sweeping statements".

"Objection sustained. Please take note, Prosecutor Sir," Judge Veeru instructed, biting his tongue as he realized it had slipped his mind that CI. Naresh was not his boss today.

"Well, Madam Warden, there are complaints that you are mistreating the inmates. Your hospitality is bordering on inhuman at times. You are not demonstrating the basic qualities of a warden. What do you have to say in defense?" the public prosecutor asked.

"As a warden, I am responsible for maintaining law and order on the campus. I cannot be lax in my duties to deliver this primary goal. It is true that I have been harsh on some inmates at times, but it was never bordering on inhuman methods," Warden Madam began to explain but was interrupted by the public prosecutor.

"Can you please elaborate on these 'methods' to the judge here? Can we also know if there is any standardized and codified treatment to ensure the equitable application of the law? Let the Judge decide on the magnitude of the treatment," CI. Naresh pressed.

Dr. Prathima took a deep breath before responding. "Your honor, our methods are designed to enforce discipline and encourage reflection among the inmates. We use a combination of isolation, manual labor, and counseling sessions. The isolation periods are meant for introspection, while manual labor helps instill a sense of responsibility and hard work. Counseling sessions are conducted to address personal issues and guide the inmates towards better behavior".

She paused, gauging the court's reaction. "We do have standardized procedures to ensure these methods are applied equitably. Each inmate's progress is monitored, and adjustments are made based on their behavior and needs. Our goal is not to inflict harm but to facilitate genuine transformation and rehabilitation. Regarding the methods, Dr. Praveen can explain that I am not an authority in her subject".

Judge Veeru listened intently, considering her words. "Thank you, Dr. Prathima. We will take your explanation into account as we continue to evaluate the practices here".

"Thanks, Madam Warden. You can take leave. We will call you again if necessary," the public prosecutor turned to the judge. With your permission, can I request Dr. Praveena in the witness box?"

As soon as Judge Veeru granted permission, Dr. Praveena, draped perfectly in a saree exuding elegance and confidence, walked briskly to the witness box. The supervisor's voice choked as he attempted to call her by name. She is usually referred to as Madam Doctor and is regarded by the inmates with a mix of respect and fear.

Dr. Praveena took her place in the witness box, ready to face the following questions. The room fell silent, the air thick with anticipation.

"Hello, Madam. Good afternoon. Can I know more about your education? Are your certificates genuine? Sorry for asking this, but many quacks deliver medical tips on YouTube and WhatsApp. Please prove that you are not one of them," the public prosecutor initiated his probe.

"Well, I am a registered and qualified practitioner. I can show my IIMA registration to prove my certification. Your intention to check the veracity of my certification is highly appreciated," replied Dr. Praveena.

"Thanks for clarifying. Can you please explain the controversial treatment methods you employ here? We would like to know why such harsh methods are employed and why," the public prosecutor continued, probing into the methods to prove they are irrational and inhumane.

"Thank you for your questions, Prosecutor. Firstly, I want to clarify that all the treatment methods we employ here are based on established medical principles and are designed to facilitate recovery and rehabilitation. Here are some key points to consider:

Evidence-Based Practices: Our methods are rooted in evidence-based practices that are widely accepted in the medical community. This includes cognitive-behavioral therapy (CBT), which is used to help individuals recognize and change destructive thought patterns.

Comprehensive Care: We provide a holistic approach to treatment. This means we address not just the mental health needs of the individuals, but also their physical, social, and occupational well-being. For example, the combination of manual labor and counseling sessions is designed to instill a sense of responsibility and help the individuals regain their self-esteem and life skills.

Ethical Standards: All our procedures adhere to the ethical standards set by medical regulatory bodies. We have regular reviews and audits to ensure compliance with these standards. Any treatment deemed harmful or unethical is immediately discontinued.

Individualized Treatment Plans: Each inmate receives a personalized treatment plan tailored to their specific needs. This plan is developed after a thorough assessment by our team of qualified professionals, including psychiatrists, psychologists, and social workers.

Progress Monitoring and Adjustment: We continuously monitor the progress of each individual and make necessary adjustments to their treatment plans. This ensures that the methods remain effective and do not cause undue harm.

Transparency and Accountability: We maintain transparency in our operations and are open to scrutiny. Regular reports and documentation of our methods and outcomes are available for review.

Positive Outcomes: We have numerous cases where individuals have successfully reintegrated into society after completing our programs. These success stories highlight the efficacy of our treatment methods and the positive impact on the lives of those we serve.

"Thanks, Madam. We are specifically referring to your 'Pupae treatment' in the dark room. Can you be very specific about this treatment and whether it is an approved medical practice?" the public prosecutor highlighted the method under investigation.

Dr. Praveena took a deep breath before responding. "The 'Pupae treatment' is a method we use to encourage deep introspection and self-reflection. It involves placing individuals in a dark, quiet room for a set period, allowing them to confront their thoughts and emotions without external distractions. This method is designed to help them process their past actions and understand the impact of their behavior on themselves and others".

She continued, "While this method is not a standard practice in conventional psychiatric treatment, it is inspired by therapeutic techniques that emphasize mindfulness and self-awareness. We ensure that the duration and conditions of the treatment are carefully monitored to prevent any harm. Our goal is to facilitate a transformative experience that leads to genuine rehabilitation".

Dr. Praveena looked at the judge and said, "Your honor, we understand that this method may seem unconventional, but it is implemented with the utmost care and consideration for the well-being of the individuals. We have seen positive outcomes from this approach, and it is always conducted under strict supervision. I also submit to this court that there is no method here that employs corporal punishment as a means of treatment."

"That's all I have at present, your honor," the public prosecutor said, taking leave and allowing the defendant to take the stage.

The judge turned to Dr. Ramesh in the capacity of the defendant and asked if he wanted to cross-examine the witness or any other person.

"Thank you, your honor. I want to cross-examine CI. Naresh." The courtroom buzzed with interest as the public prosecutor turned witness for a moment.

CI. Naresh removed his cap and stepped into the witness box to face the questions.

"Thanks for accepting the request. Can you please tell the court about the batch you graduated from at the State Police Academy? Can you also share your career trajectory, including your highs and lows?" Dr. Ramesh asked.

"Your honor, how is this relevant to the case? I am not obliged to answer anything unrelated to the matter at hand," CI. Naresh replied, declining to answer unrelated questions.

"Your honor, it is related. It is relevant because CI. Naresh's early career was marred by controversial episodes, including the custodial death of a person 'sub judice.' I am not interested in discussing any other topic. We can focus on that particular episode if he agrees," the defendant pointedly referred to a specific incident in CI. Naresh's career".

"The case you are referring to is closed, and I have received my share of punishment for it. I missed two promotion cycles and had to work under one of my juniors. Since then, I have stopped using harsh methods. That episode actually helped me in my career, as I focused on other techniques to gather evidence and catch criminals. It is difficult to assess an individual's tolerance to corporal punishment," CI. Naresh explained from the witness box.

"It changed you for the better. Now, please tell us about your experience with reformation. Based on your experience, which technique between self-realization and fear has a higher success rate?" the defendant probed further into CI. Naresh's experiences.

"Self-realization certainly has the highest success rate as the reformation starts from the inner self. It begins with realization and ends with self-correction. This method lasts longer and is fuelled by positive reinforcement from family and society. Corporal punishment, at best, teaches a person to find ways to evade it. In India, we have experimented with open prisons and achieved commendable success in reforming hardened criminals. The walls of these estates are not eight feet tall like our farmhouse. Inmates are encouraged to pick up a trade for a living and are trained under experts. They are certified to have a second chance to live a fulfilling life," CI. Naresh explained, drawing from his experience.

Dr. Ramesh then asked, "What prevents people from 'Realizing'?"

CI. Naresh took a moment before answering, "Several factors can prevent people from reaching self-realization. It often stems from deep-seated denial, fear, and a lack of self-awareness. Many individuals fear facing their flaws and mistakes because it's painful and requires significant effort to change. Additionally, societal pressures and negative influences can hinder personal growth. Without the right environment and support, it's challenging for someone to embark on the path of self-realization".

"Above all, it's the environment you are in and the distractions that setup poses. As long as a person is in the same environment, surrounded by the same people, one cannot expect a different result. For someone to truly realize and change, they need to be transplanted to a different environment, a place of solitude where they can speak to themselves without distractions. A farmhouse provides that ambiance.

People who arrive here in an inebriated condition, though initially confused, soon adapt to this new environment. We use psychotropic medications to help manage their depression. If necessary, we employ the 'Pupa' technique," Dr. Ramesh explained, momentarily forgetting he was a defendant and speaking as if he were a witness justifying the methods.

"Thanks, CI. Naresh. You may take your seat." The defendant then turns to the Judge, asking for permission to present some success stories. The AV equipment is readied, and the window blinds are closed, creating the ambiance of a movie theatre.

The defendant places a thumb drive and explores the folder with some videos. He starts playing a few of them.

Video #1:

"Hi, my name is Shankar. I hail from a village in North India. I belong to the lowest income group, and my father is a first-generation migrant worker. In my village, I was considered 'Naalayak' because I couldn't be a worthy asset to my family or society. Addiction offered me solace for a brief period, but I spent my days dreaming only to be rudely awakened by reality.

One day, I landed at this place inebriated. The people here greeted me warmly and treated me well, compelling me to reciprocate. Dr. Praveena and Dr. Prathima are very strict, but their strictness is purposeful—to reform people like us. Dr. Natraj is both our guide and friend.

I learned carpentry here and am now applying for a job in Dubai. After earning well, I plan to meet my family once I return from Dubai. My fight is not just to rebrand myself as 'Laayak' but to truly live up to the expectations of my mentors. Thanks to the supervisor community and all the members of the NL2L farmhouse. I miss you all a lot."

Video #2:

"Hi, my name is Vikram. I come from a wealthy family. I landed here in a semi-coma state after being heavily drugged. I must have been one of the toughest patients the team here has dealt with. Born with a silver spoon and raised with privilege, I failed to realize the importance of relationships, values, and morals in our culture.

Dr. Ramesh has truly awakened my inner voice by asking questions that required deep thought. Through this process, I discovered my potential to write movie scripts. Thanks to the NL2L, who sponsored courses in my field of interest and helped me build a career, I am now working towards a brighter future.

I plan to meet my parents once I achieve something significant and ask for their pardon. I am sure they will be happy to see their son finally accomplish something in his life".

After the last video is played, the lights are switched on, and the window blinds are opened, revealing a new figure seated on the defendant's side—none other than DSP. Prathyush Reddy.

Home Guard Veeru jumps from his chair and joins CI. Naresh in saluting their boss. Veeru looks frightened as DSP. Prathyush notices the robes he is wearing. "Sorry, Sir, I was playing this role as instructed by CI Sir," Veeru said, trying to shift the blame in fear of retribution.

"I trust the judging ability of my team. Continue in that role, Veeru, and judge impartially, without bias, with your conscience," DSP. Prathyush Reddy instructed before taking a seat among the benches.

"With permission, I would like to connect online with some of our alumni who are willing to share their experiences, which may provide valuable insight for this case, your honor," Dr. Ramesh requested.

Judge Veeru considered for a moment before responding, "Yes, please proceed. We should hear the testimonials of those who have successfully reintegrated with their families." After ensuring the witnesses were not influenced and their statements were candid, he granted permission.

Dr. Ramesh then connected to a person on WhatsApp, syncing it to the TV screen for everyone to see. After a brief ring, the call was answered.

"Hello, Sir. How are you?" the person on the screen responded.

"Hi, Chiranjeev. Thanks for taking the call. I am reaching out from our Institute. Our judge here would like to hear about your transformation story. May I hand over the call?" Dr. Ramesh asked.

"Of course, Sir. I'm happy to help the institute in any way I can. I'm ready to speak," Chiranjeev replied.

CI Naresh took the phone on behalf of Judge Veeru and began, "So, Chiranjeev, please tell the court how you ended up at the institution."

"Sir, like many others, I was introduced to the institution in a state of inebriation. It's rare for someone in such a condition to come here willingly. There seems to be a guiding force that brings lucky individuals to this place. By the time we wake up from our stupor, the faces of those who brought us here are just a blur," Chiranjeev began.

"So, technically, you were kidnapped. Can we conclude it that way?" CI Naresh probed, attempting to steer the narrative.

"No, Sir, it cannot be classified as a kidnapping," Chiranjeev responded firmly. "We were not able to consent when we were picked up. Since they did not know my home, they took me to theirs. It was more like welcoming a guest who is otherwise ignored by society. I would not call it a kidnapping."

"Okay then. How long did it take for you to rejoin your family, and what was the alias you used during the interim period?" CI Naresh quizzed, keen to understand Chiranjeev's reformation journey.

"Sir, I spent three months transitioning through the initial stage, which we call the 'Pupae stage.' Once I stabilized and identified a trade that interested me, earning a certification took another eight months. Then I spent an additional six months interning under a senior plumber. When I had saved enough capital to support myself and was fully rehabilitated, I reunited with my family. You could say I spent eighteen months living under an alias," Chiranjeev explained.

"Weren't you deprived of your identity? Isn't this a basic Human Rights violation?" CI Naresh questioned, pressing for clarity.

Chiranjeev responded thoughtfully, "With due respect, Sir, many Rohingyas, illegal Bangladeshis, and other people of various nationalities live under aliases in our country. As for the identity crisis, I suffered from that stigma long before I joined this institution. This institution gave me an identity and the skills to live meaningfully. I don't believe there is any Human Rights violation. Although I might be illiterate in legal terms, I would never compare this institution to terrorist organizations that exploit people for their political gains in the name of religion."

Seeing that the public prosecutor was searching for other avenues of investigation, Dr. Ramesh stood up and intervened, "Your honor, we are partnered with reputable institutions providing ITI skills that are crucial for our society. We have an abundance of engineers who lack practical skills, like tightening a screw, but here, we offer certification courses that our butterflies can choose from. The only difference is that they pay their dues by working on the farm. This creates a symbiotic relationship between the parties."

Judge Veeru, after ensuring that the public prosecutor had exhausted all his questions and was satisfied with the answers, announced, "We will reassemble after lunch exactly at 2:00 p.m.," striking the mallet to adjourn the session. This pause was a strategic move to buy time and discuss the case with DSP Prathyush Reddy and CI Naresh, aiming for a collaborative approach.

As the courtroom began to empty, Veeru, DSP. Prathyush, and CI. Naresh gathered quietly to review the proceedings and plan their next steps.

It had been almost 24 hours, and nothing had been heard from CI. Naresh. The Head Constable checked with Madam, but there was no news there either. Growing discomfort spread about his absence, especially given that he had left fully armed. No one knew anything about the mission, the location, or whether he was part of a wider team. In his 40-year career, the Head Constable had seen some seniors vanish under the guise of a mission to relax and rewind, but CI. Naresh was not of that nature.

The Head Constable went to the CDA's desk in the cooler part of the station to check whether he was tracking the device. The CDA was relaxing.

The Head Constable instructed the CDA, "Are you tracking the device? Where are the coordinates now? Can you bring up the application? Let me see for myself."

The CDA, in return, asked, "Have you received any SoS message from him? Why didn't you tell me? Show me the message." The CDA quickly circled back with a query. "We are commanded to track only after receiving the SoS message, not before," he comforted the Head Constable, saying that the mission might be taking longer than usual. "He must be part of a larger team. Don't worry, he is safe."

"How can you be so sure of his safety? You're speaking as if you are with him and know everything about the mission. Did CI Sir give away any details of the mission?" the Head Constable began doubting the sincerity of the CDA.

While they were discussing this seriously, the phone rang, and HC rushed to pick it up, sensitive to any signal now.

"This is CI Ashok. Where is CI. Naresh? Has he switched off his phone?" HC heard the rough tone of another senior in the department.

Passing on a salute to CI Ashok over the phone, HC debriefed, "Sir, he is not in the station, and we are also unable to reach him. He clearly went on some mission but did not divulge much detail. He was tense as one of our Home Guards went missing. It appears that CI. Naresh is in hot pursuit of that case. When I spoke to Madam CI, she mentioned a search party to locate and save the missing Home Guard. I did not know that Veeru had rejoined after canceling his leave and was on a mission until Madam CI divulged this information".

"What? What mission? Let me check if he has informed the DSP about this. You keep trying to reach him and report to me immediately once you get in touch," CI Ashok commanded, putting down the phone with a heavy thud, clearly disgusted with CI. Naresh's independent actions and disregard for protocols.

CI Ashok then tried to reach the DSP, but his phone was also not reachable. He contacted the DSP's office, only to be informed that the DSP had left for a mission alone, without his protocol team. This revelation further disappointed CI Ashok, highlighting the proximity between his subordinate and his superior, which is a clear deviation from the Chain of command.

People interacted with each other while food was served buffet style. They were busy discussing and sharing opinions on the proceedings so far. The atmosphere was filled with anticipation about the outcome of the judgment.

Veeru gained courage and moved close to DSP. Prathyush, speaking softly, "Sir, with you around here, you should take the judge's seat. I don't know why CI. Naresh Sir chose me for this role. I am not a qualified judge and have no precedents for this kind of work. Please relieve me from this job," he pleaded, his voice filled with desperation.

DSP. Prathyush looked at Veeru with a stern but understanding gaze. "Veeru, I understand your concerns. But CI. Naresh must have seen something in you, a potential you might not yet recognize in yourself. Trust in his judgment and your own abilities. Continue with your duty, and you will find the strength within".

"Are you satisfied with the progress so far? Have you listened to everyone diligently? Are the responses provided by the witnesses convincing? Is there any reason to doubt whether the respondents have been influenced or coerced?" DSP. Prathyush asked Veeru, keen to ensure the integrity and quality of the judgment that was about to be delivered.

Veeru took a deep breath before responding, "Yes, Sir, I have listened carefully to all the testimonies. The responses have been thorough and convincing. I have not observed any signs of coercion or undue influence on the witnesses. I believe we are ready to proceed with a fair and just decision."

DSP. Prathyush nodded in approval, "Very well. Proceed with confidence, Veeru. Your judgment here will reflect your integrity and dedication to justice. When you find yourself in a predicament, follow your heart. You may have already observed that this institution succeeds in areas where we struggle with transformation".

CI. Naresh joined DSP. Prathyush with an element of surprise on his face. "I cannot believe that you are part of this scheme. It is even more mystifying to choose me for this job. I am thoroughly confused. Should I expect more surprises?" he asked, his voice tinged with disbelief and curiosity.

DSP. Prathyush gave a faint smile. "Naresh, sometimes the best way to accomplish our goals is to keep a few cards close to our chest. Your skills and integrity are the reasons you were chosen for this mission. Trust the process and trust yourself. There might be more surprises along the way, but they are all part of the plan to achieve our larger objective. When you are in a dilemma, follow your heart".

With his plate half full, Dr. Ramesh joined DSP. Prathyush, who was speaking with Dr. Praveena and Dr. Prathima. Dr. Prathima raised a crucial point, "One thing that is still open is the evidence of the logistics or supply chain details of bringing the junkies here. Should we disclose this last secret, potentially endangering our operations?"

DSP. Prathyush considered the question carefully. "Disclosing such details could compromise the safety and effectiveness of our operations. However, transparency is key to gaining trust and legitimacy. We need to weigh the risks and benefits carefully. Perhaps we can provide a general overview that assures the court of our ethical practices without revealing specific logistics that could jeopardize our mission".

Dr. Ramesh nodded, "It's a delicate balance. We need to show that we operate within legal and ethical boundaries while protecting the integrity of our methods".

CI. Naresh quietly approached Butterfly101, whom he had interrogated earlier in the day. "It was nice talking to you. I have developed a huge respect for you upon hearing about your transformation journey. But one thing is bothering me. Why are you so forgetful about the atrocities you were subjected to? Are you offering pardon, or are you simply unaware of the crimes these people are committing?" CI. Naresh asked, hoping to elicit a response tinged with a hint of revenge.

Butterfly101 looked thoughtfully at CI. Naresh, before responding, said, "The journey of transformation is complex. It's not about forgetting or ignoring the past atrocities. It's about finding a way to heal and move forward. Holding onto anger and resentment can consume you and hinder your progress. By choosing to focus on my personal growth and the positives in my life now, I can leave behind the pain and use my experience to help others. Please do not harbor hope of using our shoulders to fire your bullets. It will not be successful,"

Butterfly101 responded firmly, stating that they would not be manipulated or used for revenge".

"The court session shall begin in ten minutes. Please assemble in the courtroom," the bench clerk announced, tapering off all conversations in the makeshift dining space. The inmates of the farmhouse began filling the spaces, taking their seats exactly as they had in the forenoon session.

Judge Veeru sought permission to continue, marking the session open. "Before we proceed, I want to ask both the public prosecutor and the defendant if they have any other questions for witnesses or any additional evidence to present. Let's start with the public prosecutor."

"Thank you, your honor. I have one question for all the butterflies here. If there is even one person who feels victimized by the act of kidnap, please stand up. This is your last chance to get justice. Please stand against the perpetrators, and I will fully protect you of my abilities," the CI asked, facing the audience with anticipation, hoping for at least one person to come forward.

CI. Naresh interpreted the lack of response as a positive outcome for the institution and the dedicated individuals whose services have been recognized by the microcosm of people who have benefited from securing a second chance for a better life.

"I have one request for Dr. Ramesh, your honor. I would like the complete list of the Butterflies, their status, and the aliases they are living under. This will help us connect with their families and conclude the open cases.

I believe he shouldn't have any objections to this," CI. Naresh stated clearly, addressing the court.

"Your honor, we will provide access to all the butterflies who are alumni of this institution and are living with alternate identities until they achieve something valued by their families. They do not want to reunite until such time. It is important to value their sentiments as they are working towards erasing the brand of 'Naalaayaks.' Once they decide to reunite with their families, we will approach CI. Naresh directly," stated Dr. Ramesh.

Judge Veeru then hints at the defendant, "I do not have anything to ask or present, your honor," confirmed Dr. Ramesh.

Alignment To The Vision

"DSP, Sir, we would like to hear your closing remarks before the court delivers its verdict." Veeru requests that DSP speak to the audience here.

DSP. Prathyush stood up, addressing the courtroom with a composed demeanor. "Thank you, Veeru. This case and the testimonies we have heard today highlight the profound impact that dedication and compassion can have on individuals' lives. The transformation we have witnessed among the butterflies speaks volumes about the effectiveness of the institution and the commitment of those who work tirelessly to give these individuals a second chance.

Our goal should always be to rehabilitate and reintegrate people into society as responsible and dignified citizens. The path is challenging and requires unwavering faith in human potential. However, the rewards are immeasurable when we see individuals reclaim their lives and contribute positively to their communities.

I urge everyone here to continue supporting and believing in these efforts. Let this court's decision reflect not just the letter of the law but also the spirit of justice and humanity. Thank you."

"DSP. Prathyush continued, "I joined the police force four decades ago. Over the years, we have witnessed significant transformations in maintaining law and order. We've learned from our mistakes and improved our practices. While we have apprehended many criminals and, in some cases, eliminated threats, true transformation always eluded us.

This initiative was Natraj and my brainchild. As close friends, we share a common vision and purpose. It brings me immense satisfaction to see this vision materialize successfully, achieving something that wasn't possible through traditional methods. I am proud to retire knowing that we have made a lasting, positive impact on people's lives."

Judge Veeru then asks CI. Naresh to deliver his closing remarks.

CI. Naresh stood up, addressing the courtroom with a steady voice. "Ladies and gentlemen, as we reach the end of these proceedings, I want to express my gratitude to everyone who has participated in this important case. Over the past few days, we have heard remarkable testimonies and witnessed the profound impact that this institution has had on countless lives.

Our mission in law enforcement has always been to uphold justice, protect the innocent, and maintain order. However, true justice is not only about punishment but also about rehabilitation and transformation. What we have seen here is a testament to the power of second chances and the incredible potential for change within every individual.

Part III: The Butterflies

I stand here today, not just as an officer of the law but as a firm believer in the capacity for human growth and redemption. The dedication and compassion shown by the people who run this institution have opened my eyes to new possibilities and methods in our pursuit of justice.

Let us remember that our ultimate goal is to create a society where every individual has the opportunity to thrive and contribute positively. This institution has set a remarkable example, and I hope we can all take its lessons to heart as we move forward.

Thank you."

"Dr. Ramesh, the court would like to hear your remarks as well before we break," requests Judge Veeru.

Dr. Ramesh stood up, his voice steady and filled with conviction. "Your honor, esteemed colleagues, and community members, today marks a significant milestone in our journey of rehabilitation and transformation. Our institution has always believed in the power of second chances and the inherent potential within every individual to change for the better.

Over the course of these proceedings, we have seen firsthand the incredible progress and resilience of those we serve. Their stories of transformation are not just personal victories but a testament to the collective efforts of everyone involved in this mission.

Our approach is built on compassion, support, and unwavering belief in human dignity. We understand that the path to redemption is difficult but achievable with the right guidance and encouragement. As we move forward, I urge all of us to continue fostering an environment where every individual can rebuild their lives and contribute positively to society.

Remember that true justice is about punishment, restoration, and healing. Together, we can create a brighter future for everyone. Thank you."

After hearing all members' concluding remarks, Judge Veeru announced, "We will take a two-hour break to prepare the verdict. Let's reconvene at 5:30 p.m. when the court will deliver its decision."

The attendees slowly dispersed, some heading to the makeshift dining area while others chose to gather in small groups to discuss the implications of the day's proceedings. The anticipation hung in the air as everyone eagerly awaited the final verdict.

Part III: The Butterflies

Justice Delivered

It was nearing forty-eight hours, and there was still no SoS from CI. Naresh. Home Guard Veeru's phone was also untraceable. The Head Constable, feeling a growing sense of urgency, went to the CDA's table in the adjacent room, only to find the chair empty and a letter on the table, anchored by a glass marble, gently waving under the light breeze.

With a sense of foreboding, the Head Constable picked up the letter and read the contents:

"To,

CI. Naresh Sir,

My work here is over. I hope your mission is successful and meaningful. I take my leave, Sir.

Many Thanks.

Yours, Butterfly"

"What work? What mission? What's this alias Butterfly?" The Head Constable's mind was spinning. He immediately called CI Ashok to inform him about the missing CDA.

"What CDA? I have never heard about this role or position. Are you allowing some charlatans to infiltrate our department? Send me his appointment letter so I can check with the Personnel department," CI Ashok responded, clearly agitated.

The Head Constable quickly searched for the CDA's appointment letter, which was meticulously filed but now missing. He then tried to surf for photos of the CDA but found none on his phone. Panic began to set in as he realized something far more complex and mysterious was at play.

He racked his brain, trying to recall any detail that could provide a clue. The air was thick with tension as he considered his next steps. It was becoming increasingly clear that this case was unlike any other he had encountered in his long career.

The CDA vanished as smoothly as he had entered. He was the mole who had created the perfect ambiance, even crafting an alias email ID that mimicked the department's official ID, allowing him to access the Criminal Database. The full extent of the damage done was unknown. The Head Constable informed CI Ashok, only to be reprimanded.

CI Ashok quickly formed a search party and started the survey from the police station. He also alerted the sniffer dogs team as three members of the police department had gone missing within forty-eight hours.

CI Ashok began his investigation in CI. Naresh's chamber. He found a piece of paper on which a 16-digit number was scribbled. The Head Constable suddenly remembered that the number belonged to a tracking device that had been given to the imposter CDA, which was to be tracked on Apple AirTag®.

With CI. Naresh's location detected and his movement confined to a few hundred square feet, the team felt a sense of relief. CI Ashok took permission to form a rescue team comprising a hundred constables drawn from the city to ensure a successful operation.

The police caravan started moving towards the coordinates shown in the app, with CI Ashok leading in the pilot vehicle and keeping a continuous view of the map. The tension was palpable as the team prepared for the rescue mission and determined to bring CI. Naresh and possibly Home Guard back safely.

Part III: The Butterflies

Everyone gathered in the Courtroom upon hearing the call by the Bench Clerk.

Everyone took a seat after the Judge had taken his seat.

The following judgment is delivered.

"This judgment is to be signed by every stakeholder here and promise to this court that it will be upheld in spirit. Delivering judgment is one, and its implementation is another challenge." The judge takes the confirmation from the members in the room.

Judgment dated 4th December 2024.

In the case brought before this honorable court, we have meticulously examined the evidence presented and heard the testimonies of all relevant parties. This court acknowledges the complexity and sensitivity of the issues at hand, which involve the rehabilitation and transformation of individuals who have previously engaged in criminal activities.

The institution in question has demonstrated a profound commitment to providing second chances and facilitating the reintegration of these individuals into society as responsible and dignified citizens. The testimonies provided by the butterflies—individuals who have undergone significant personal growth and transformation—are a testament to the effectiveness and impact of the institution's efforts.

Dr. Ramesh, along with his dedicated team, has showcased a model of compassion, support, and unwavering belief in human dignity. Their approach, which balances strict adherence to ethical standards and innovative rehabilitation methods, has resulted in the successful transformation of numerous individuals. This court commends the institution for its groundbreaking work and the positive outcomes it has achieved.

However, the court is also mindful of the concerns raised regarding the confidentiality and safety of the individuals involved. The institution's practice of allowing these individuals to assume alternate identities until they feel ready to reunite with their families is both innovative and necessary for their continued well-being and personal growth. This practice is a crucial component of the rehabilitation process and must be respected.

This court also takes into consideration the concerns raised by CI. Naresh regarding the potential misuse of the institution's resources and the need for transparency in its operations. It is imperative that any program operating within the judicial system adheres to the highest standards of integrity and accountability.

Therefore, the court issues the following directives:

1. **Transparency and Accountability**: The institution must maintain comprehensive records of all individuals under its care and provide periodic updates to the relevant authorities. These records should include the progress of the individuals, their current status, and any changes in their identities, ensuring that the process remains transparent and accountable.

2. **Protection of Identities:** While the institution must be transparent in its operations, it is equally

important to protect the identities of the individuals undergoing rehabilitation. The institution should implement robust measures to ensure that their alternate identities are not compromised and that their privacy is maintained until they are ready to reunite with their families.

3. **Collaboration with Law Enforcement:** The institution must collaborate closely with law enforcement agencies to ensure that any individuals who pose a potential threat to society are appropriately monitored and managed. This collaboration should also facilitate the resolution of any outstanding cases involving these individuals.

4. **Continued Support and Guidance:** The institution should continue to provide comprehensive support and guidance to individuals undergoing rehabilitation. This includes psychological counseling, vocational training, and any other resources necessary to aid their successful reintegration into society.

5. **Periodic Review:** The court mandates periodic reviews of the institution's practices and outcomes to ensure that its methods remain effective and aligned with the principles of justice and rehabilitation. These reviews should be conducted by an independent body to maintain objectivity and fairness.

In conclusion, this court recognizes the tremendous efforts and successes of the institution in transforming lives and upholding the values of justice and humanity.

Part III: The Butterflies

We urge all parties involved to continue their dedication to this noble cause, ensuring that every individual is given the opportunity to rebuild their life and contribute positively to society.

The court will reconvene in six months to review the progress and ensure compliance with these directives.

Signed by

Dr. Ramesh

CI. Naresh

DSP. Prathyush

Dr. Praveena

Dr. Prathima

As witnessed by:

All Supervisors, Inmates, and attendees of this court session.

As the final judgment was delivered, the mallet echoed through the courtroom, marking the session's conclusion. The atmosphere was filled with a sense of accomplishment and hope. The butterflies, the institution's team, and the law enforcement officers left the courtroom with renewed purpose and determination to continue their transformative journey.

Dr. Ramesh's walkie-talkie hissed to life, and the voice of the perimeter security alerted the inmates about the flood of police vehicles approaching. Dr. Ramesh immediately ordered, "Open the main gates and let in the police party. We have more guests today than usual."

As the police caravan rolled in, CI Ashok noticed DSP. Prathyush and decided to mellow down the criticality of the rescue mission. The tension in the air seemed to ease slightly as the officers disembarked from their vehicles and prepared to enter the institution.

DSP. Prathyush approached Dr. Ramesh, "It seems we have a full house today. Let's ensure everything proceeds smoothly and without incident."

Dr. Ramesh nodded, "Absolutely. We're all here to ensure the safety and well-being of everyone involved."

Part III: The Butterflies

With the commotion brought under control, CI Naresh asked Veeru to return home and prepare for his balance exams. The Head Constable marked Veeru as present, duly approved by CI Naresh.

CI Naresh was the go-to officer for closing missing person cases and aiding in reuniting the butterflies with their families. His dedication to these cases earned him numerous accolades and out-of-turn promotions. His exemplary work reflected his commitment to justice and his approval of this offbeat method of the rehabilitation program. Sometimes, remaining silent allows justice to be delivered in many unknown forms, showing that unconventional methods can lead to profound and positive societal changes.

The institution's approach to rehabilitation is unique and transformative. While individuals may arrive at the institution under unusual circumstances, the focus is on providing them with a safe and supportive environment where they can rebuild their lives. The program offers comprehensive counseling, vocational training, and community support, enabling participants to successfully develop valuable skills and reintegrate into society. The institution's commitment to upholding human dignity and providing second chances has led to numerous success stories, demonstrating the profound impact of compassionate rehabilitation.

DSP Prathyush approved the promotion of CI Naresh in the next cycle, recognizing his exceptional leadership and dedication. Additionally, he nominated Naresh for a gallantry award, acknowledging his demonstration of care and safety for his team members, even at the risk of his own life.

CI Naresh returned to the police station and handed over all the bullets, symbolizing the success of a mission accomplished without firing a single shot. It was a testament to the power of strategic planning, collaboration, and non-violent conflict resolution, marking a significant achievement in his career and setting a powerful example for his colleagues.

"SARVEJANA SUKHINOBHAVANTU"

About The Author

An Indian upper-middle-class individual grew up the social ladder by toiling, paying taxes, fearing God, and not breaking a single rule: a devout Hindu, an empathetic individual, and a patriot.

I graduated in Agricultural Sciences, so I have a glimpse of Rural exposure, though it is dated. I have been an Urbanite by birth and all my life. I am a postgraduate in business management and working at an Indian IT MNC.

I recently started to pursue my hobbies. I grew up reading Panchatantra and Chandamama comics, so I developed a skill for hearing the unheard.

Likes travel, driving, and watching YouTube to keep abreast of Geopolitics.

Synopsis:

In a gripping tale of justice and redemption, the story follows CI. Naresh, DSP. Prathyush, and Dr. Ramesh as they navigate the complexities of transforming lives through an innovative rehabilitation program. The institution, led by Dr. Ramesh, provides second chances to former offenders, helping them reintegrate into society under new identities as "butterflies."

As the story unfolds, a court case brought against the institution examines its methods and successes. Through the testimonies of the transformed individuals, or "butterflies," the institution's impact is laid bare, showcasing the power of compassion and support in rehabilitation.

CI. Naresh and Home Guard Veeru work undercover to expose the threats and ensure the institution's safety. Their efforts, alongside the steadfast leadership of DSP. Prathyush, highlight the importance of collaboration between law enforcement and rehabilitation programs.

The novel culminates in a suspenseful courtroom verdict that validates the institution's mission while emphasizing transparency, accountability, and protection for those undergoing rehabilitation. The story concludes with a powerful message of hope, transformation, and the enduring belief in human potential.

www.ingramcontent.com/pod-product-compliance
Lightning Source LLC
LaVergne TN
LVHW041712070526
838199LV00045B/1316